Sharptooth

Mika Horvath

Pepperback Press, Inc.

A note...

Dear Reader,

I have a secret. Are you ready? Brace yourself...

Sharptooth is a vampire!

Had you guessed? Did you know my secret? I think it's a pretty good one. After all, even Sharptooth didn't know.

But really, she should have at least suspected. After all, normal little girls don't run through the forest looking for squirrels to eat.

And that's really what I wanted to chat with you about. The squirrels. The bunnies. Other fuzzy little things—but not the skunks, obviously. Also, there's a mountain lion. And a bad guy who is somewhat worse for wear at the end.

This book is just a little...bloody.

Well, she is a vampire, after all.

So, dear reader, as much as I want everyone to know Sharptooth's story, please consider if this is the right book for *you*.

Neither of us, I promise, will be offended either way.

With our love,
Mika and Sharptooth

Prologue

Before she ran away, my mother taught me to read and write but not how to braid my long, black hair. Now it follows behind me like a cape as I run through the night.

When I'm hungry I chase the small warm things. I'm very, very fast.

Maybe my mother didn't run away, but I'm all alone now. The windows of my house are broken and the floors are covered in dirt. Everything is black and it's always dark.

When I catch the small warm things I bite them like I bit my mother. I always try to be gentle. *Gentle*, my mother said. I bite them until my belly doesn't hurt, and then I put them back. *Gentle*.

Sometimes when I put back the small warm things they hop away. But sometimes they don't. Sometimes, before their blood has cooled, I use it to write my name in the snow.

The smallest things are the ones that don't scamper away after I bite them. They used to but I think now my bite is too big for them. I used to be able to walk under the table in my house but now I can put my elbows on top without getting up on my toes. I am bigger, and so is my bite.

My mother did not show me how to catch the small warm things. I was lying on the floor in my room, curled around the pain in my belly. It felt like there were sharp things inside of me and everything hurt. My head hurt and my fingers hurt, but it was the sharp pain in my belly that made me cry.

While I was lying on the floor, a small warm thing pitter-pattered closer and closer to me. The sharp things in my belly moved into my mouth. Suddenly my teeth were sharp. I bit the small warm thing. My sharp teeth sank through its soft fur and my belly was quiet and warm and nothing hurt. When there were no more small warm things to bite in my room, I searched through the house. When there were no more small warm things in the house, I began to run through the night.

The night is full of trees that are tall and shadows that are long. Once my mother took me into the town and we walked through the carriages and crowds of men. There were so many tall people there and they all said, "Pardon me," if they walked too close.

When I run through the trees I pretend they are tall men and I say, "Pardon me," as I fly past them.

All of the things in the trees stop and stare at me and I laugh. There are so many small warm things here for me to bite and my belly is never sharp.

My teeth are, though. Always.

I am Sharptooth.

Chapter One

Many of the surfaces in my house are black and crumble when I touch them. The black sticks to my fingers and sometimes I rub it on my legs to hide them when I run in the night. It is not easy to creep when your legs hang below your dress, glowing white like the birch trees that stand by the edge of the forest.

When I wake in my room and rise from where I was curled up on the floor, the crisp night air tickles across the skin of my back. It races in from the broken glass of the window and through the ripped side of my dress.

I frown at the torn seam and say the bad word my mother told me to never say.

With one tug the dress falls from my body. I consider the expanse of pale skin and imagine rubbing the soot from the walls all over and being done with it.

A memory blows through my mind like a storm. I was running naked through the hallway, my mother laughing as she raced after me, a bright dress clutched in her hands. Without thought, my feet take me into the next room. Here there is the husk of a large bed and a tall wood cabinet, charred and cracked.

Hanging inside the black cabinet are her dresses, their brightness untouched by the darkness. Some have ribbons and sashes and some are simple and plain, but they all are in such glorious colors that they shine like jewels in the moonlight.

I run my hands over the first one and smile. Even in the dark, the yellow shimmers and the fabric flows like water across my fingers. My mother dances across my memories, draped in this soft sunshine and laughing, her eyes tilted up to the sky. The next dress crinkles at my touch, layers of grass green that are stiff and full of tiny little holes. As I stroke over the pattern, I see my mother walking with a basket on her arm, then sitting in the sun with tears in her eyes. The last dress is tucked back behind the others and it is as black as the charred wood. I don't remember my mother ever wearing this dress.

It takes me a very, very long time to get into the black dress and I say the bad word more than once. I wiggle and turn until the bright white of my skin is mostly hidden by the dress that falls to my ankles and I am finally ready to run through the night.

From outside of my house my friend Shadow yips impatiently. Sometimes he sleeps curled against my back, but often I wake and I am alone. I think I remember the line of light opening like a snake's eye as he pushes out of the door, but maybe those are dreams.

"Good day, m'lord," I say as I walk into the night. I curtsy before him in my long dress like my mother did. Shadow cocks his head at me and my laughter launches the birds into the air.

Shadow lets his jaw drop and his tongue hang down, his tail wagging madly. When he was born, he was so much bigger than his mother's other babies. Now Shadow is three times the size of any other wolf in the forest. His mother had many litters, every year after the snows had melted. But then she had this single black pup, so different from the brothers and sisters who came before him.

I bound down the overgrown path and Shadow falls into step beside me. He keeps up easily as I fly through the night, our six legs flashing over the leaves with soft pats that sound like sighs. I like to hunt in the leaves. It's much more interesting than in the snow, where every step is plain to see. The leaves keep their secrets, for the most part.

Small warm things rustle in the undergrowth as we run through the trees. Occasionally a larger beast rumbles by here and there, but I don't want to stop. I know Shadow hears them too, but he stays by my side, paws eating up the distance. His long red tongue waves from his mouth and my black hair flies out behind me as we run.

We come to the edge of the trees and I still haven't found anything interesting. I burst into the tall grasses without stopping. Here the moon gets a good look at us, the girl in her long black dress and the wolf in his glossy black fur. The silver light shines down on us, approving of our matching attire. The round moon is always nice. Soon he will twist himself into a snide smile again and the small warm things in the forest will hide in his meager light.

On the darkest nights, the trees have shape but no color. This night, as the full round face of the moon looks down on us kindly, the grasses are green and yellow as they brush against the long skirt of my dress. The little purple flowers that dot the field are darker, but still not as dark as me or my Shadow.

Even the night sky isn't really black—it's blue. A deep, dark blue, full of tiny little holes of light. Shadow and I come to the top of a long, low hill covered in lush grasses. The lights in the sky are reflected below in the small town that sits in the valley. I remember the cobblestone roads and carriages, tall men in the street and the ladies in the houses with dresses in bright colors. I remember the sweet iced biscuits they'd have with tea when my mother and I would come to visit.

It's been a very long time since I've had a biscuit. Or tea. Or food of any kind, really. I bite the things I catch, and that's enough. That's not just *enough*. It's *just right.*

But it would be nice to have a biscuit.

I angle us toward the town and our fast feet take us down the hills and closer to the lights of the houses. We've never come this way before and my shoulders are tight, but Shadow stays by my side, his stride loose and his gaze straight ahead. He knows I'll find us something warm to fill our bellies.

Chapter Two

The houses give off light and the warm smells of various foods along with the sour smells of the people who eat them. We slow down as we run between the tall, dark shadows cast between them.

There.

We duck between two houses and the sweet smell of biscuits floats on the breeze. I go down one row and turn back as the scent gets fainter. Now I've got it. We come up to the back of a large house surrounded on both sides by its twins.

Through the large windows a woman in a black and white dress walks through the house with a covered tray.

I lead Shadow around to the rear of the house where a large wall blocks our view. Without thought, I leap to the top of the wall, but a faint whine brings me up short.

On the ground Shadow plops his fur-covered bottom onto the cobblestones and snaps his teeth in frustration.

"I'll be right back, " I tell him from my perch on the top of the wall.

Shadow sighs and settles into the dark corner at the base of the wall, nearly disappearing even from my sight.

I turn back to the courtyard and drop down to land behind a fat bush full of yellow roses.

"Just a little treat, Miss." A soft voice wafts through the night. "Then you'd best be in bed."

I move soundlessly around the rosebush to see a slight figure sitting on a bench. The woman sets the tray on the bench beside them and backs away, her hands clasped before her.

"It will be hours yet until my parents return home, Marie," a clear, sweet voice answers. "We'll be lucky to see them before dawn, don't you agree?"

"Be that as it may, Miss, it's still not good for your health to be out in the garden so late," comes the stern reply.

"I distinctly recall the doctor saying that fresh air was good for me."

Marie huffs at her. "I'm sure he didn't mean the *night* air, Miss Lyssa!" The woman looks scandalized by the thought. "You're going to catch a chill in your lungs on top of everything else," she muttered.

"Perhaps you should bring me my blue shaw, Marie."

Marie huffs again but nods. “Very well, Miss.”

The woman hustles back into the house, still muttering dire predictions under her breath. The slight figure on the bench lifts the cover from the tray and the scent of the biscuits is everywhere, seeping into my brain and sparking memories of afternoons in sunny rooms.

I creep forward, the scent of sugar and cream drawing me in. I move from shadow to shadow in the garden, stopping beneath another large flowering bush behind the bench holding the girl and her treasure.

Up close, I’m fascinated by the ripples the girl’s hair makes as it cascades over the back of the bench. As she lifts one of the biscuits from the tray and bites into it, saliva floods my mouth in a manner usually reserved for fluffy fat bunnies.

I pad carefully forward until I’m close enough to touch the silver ripples of her hair. I reach around them and slip my hand between the slats at the back of the bench and carefully remove a biscuit, then quickly shuffle back beneath the rose bush. It is warm. I take a tiny, tiny nibble from the biscuit, using my flat front teeth. They sink through the soft icing before hitting the spongy cookie beneath, and I nearly moan as the sugary goodness hits my tongue.

The biscuit is gone too quickly and the silly girl is sitting there with a whole tray of the beautiful treats. They look so lonely. It would be such a terrible waste not to eat them while they’re warm.

I shuffle back over to the bench and once again slip a biscuit between the slats. As I slide back into my hiding space the girl laughs into her hand. I ignore her and indulge in the ecstasy of my biscuit.

I'm contemplating another trip when the woman returns from the house carrying a length of material. I sink further into the shadows as she fusses over the girl, placing the fabric over her lap.

"I'm so pleased to see you eating, Miss Lyssa," the woman approves.

"The biscuits are lovely, Marie. Could you bring me another plate?"

"Of course! Of course! Your mother will be so happy. I'll be right back, Miss." Marie claps her hands together and hustles back into the house.

There are only two biscuits left on the plate. The girl reaches down and picks up one. The last one sits, unloved and alone. I know the risk is too great and my heart weeps.

"You may take it," the girl prompts.

I cock my head, not moving from my hiding spot.

"Quick," she urges, "before Marie returns."

Could she be talking to me?

I crouch, frozen, beneath the rose bush as Marie comes bustling back out of the house with another covered tray. The girl picks up the last biscuit as Marie switches out the plates on the bench beside her, still smiling as she returns to the house carrying the empty tray.

"Take them all," the girl says, rising slowly from the bench and walking toward the door with shuffling steps.

I sit very still, looking for the trap. My gaze moves from the doorway to the house the girl has disappeared through, across the blossom-dotted bushes of the garden, and back again to the bench. I focus on the space above the plate of biscuits where the air shimmers as their warmth rises into the cool night.

Giving into temptation I leap forward. In a second the plate is empty and I'm scaling the garden wall one-handed, the other hand clasping my treasure to my chest. Then Shadow and I are bounding through the night.

There is a place in the forest that my mother called the fairy circle. It is a quiet little bubble in the middle of all of the trees where the grass is short and soft. In the fairy circle, Shadow and I sit and share the sweet biscuits. I break each one into pieces to prolong the experience, nearly losing my fingers as I feed the tiny bits to my friend.

"Thank you so much for accepting my invitation to tea," I intone, grasping Shadow's big black paw in my hand. He cocks his head at me but doesn't pull his paw away. I give him another small piece of the biscuit and he devours it in one bite. I eat my piece with more restraint, savoring every morsel as my mind wanders back to the girl with the silver waves of hair.

Had she meant for me to take them?

Shadow bounces off into the trees. A moment later he comes trotting back with a hare dangling from his red-stained muzzle. He collapses back beside me and happily munches on his treasure while I do the same with mine.

Chapter Three

I fall asleep with a full belly but the next night I wake up starving, the sharp pains of hunger twisting inside me. My teeth and my fingertips ache with the need to hunt. Shadow isn't waiting, so I run through the trees alone, my hair flying out behind me as I jump a fallen log and startle a family of skunks. I don't stop. Some creatures aren't worth hunting.

Minutes later I pluck a small brown squirrel from a tree, its cheeks full of its harvest, and sink my teeth deep into its furred back. I am not gentle. I am hungry and this little one will not be scampering away after I've had my fill. Its body falls to the forest floor, nuts rolling from its gaping mouth.

Shadow bursts from the trees and scoops it up. The carcass is gone in a flash.

"You're quite welcome."

His long tongue unfurls from between his teeth and sways as he wags his entire body with his big fluffy tail. My laugh rings out and the birds in the trees above us take flight into the night sky.

We run through the forest, taking turns at the lead, and once again find ourselves on the outskirts of the town. I slide my eyes over to Shadow, sure he's dreaming of sweet biscuits. The moon has been out for hours and it's very late. There are no men on the street and no lights in the windows. We don't have to be careful as we run down the middle of the cobbled roads.

There are shops along each side of the street here, but they are all dark and empty. The world is always asleep when I am awake. In my memories, when I see the tall men walking up and down the streets and the ladies drinking tea and biscuits, it is always so bright.

I stop to stare into a window. When did I get switched around from everyone else?

Shadow nudges against my hip with his big muzzle, moving me away from the building. He pokes his wet nose against my side until I begin to run again, leaving my memories behind.

The house with the walled garden once again smells of sweet biscuits. The garden is empty but a tray is sitting alone on the bench, its promising mound covered by a white cloth. I slink through the shadows in the garden and sidle my way to the bench. I lift the lacy edge of the cloth and the sugary smell of the biscuits drifts up to me and I close my eyes in ecstasy.

In a moment I've scooped every biscuit off the tray and wrapped them into the cloth and I'm bounding back toward the wall with my treasure.

"Wait!" a soft voice calls out from the house.

My feet don't pause but my head whips around as I hit the top of the wall. Sitting in an open window above the garden, a slight form leans out into the night. Waves of moonlit hair spill over her shoulder as she reaches out an arm. I hold her gaze until I slip over the wall and I am hidden from her view.

Shadow prances at my side as my feet hit the bricks of the alleyway, nosing at the wrapped bundle in my arms. I take off back the way we came, my friend hot on my heels.

By the time we tumble to the grassy surface of the fairy circle, the biscuits have cooled, but they're still warmer than the night air as I unwrap them. I break the first one in half and pop one piece in my mouth while offering the other to Shadow. His piece is instantly gone but I savor my half. The creamy icing has a bit of a citrus tang to it that balances out the crumbly, buttery cookie. With only my friend and a ring of mushrooms as witness, I allow myself to moan in contentment.

The cookies are gone much too soon. In no time I am lying back on the grass, a big black head cradled on my belly, as I stare up at the moon. There are dips and valleys on the surface like scars on a cat's back .

Everything is silver and blue under the light of the moon. Sometimes I can pick out the red of the blood that runs down the back of the creatures I catch and the colors of my mother's pretty dresses. But I know this isn't what the world is supposed to look like. I remember what the colors looked like in the sun, under the bright blue sky.

Shadow falls asleep with his head nestled against me and we lay there in the fairy circle for a long time. I fight the urge to head back to my room.

Little by little the night sky begins to show different shades of purple and blue. I marvel at the colors but a ball of dread builds in my chest. It is time to go home. It is time to burrow into my nest and close my eyes. My head is heavy and my eyes become gritty and dry.

I am so tired and the sky is so big.

Shadow rouses beside me and begins whimpering. I run my hand over his head, trying to soothe us both, but he is having none of it. He stands over me and woofs from deep in his barrel chest, close to my face. It startles me. I am not scared of Shadow—but I am scared.

My determination to see the colors in the sunlight seems like the stupidest thought I'd ever had. I regret everything. Leaping to my feet I run for home as fast as I can, flying over felled trees and startling small warm things beginning to stir after the long night.

Above me the sky has lightened to a color between gray and blue and purple, like a stone slab dangling over my head. I hold the long black skirts of my mother's dress up high and my pale legs flash over the ground in a blur.

I break through the trees and the hill between me and my house is edged in a pink light. A spark appears at the crest of the hill and my body is filled with a burning pain. I go tumbling to the ground.

The need to return to my nest is overtaken by a need to get away–to get away from the sky. Instinct rides me as I begin to dig down into the dirt. My black nails become thicker and longer as they claw at the ground. I have barely made a dent into the fresh soil when something hits me from behind. My face plants into the cool, damp earth and the pain is gone. My mind drifts away to the sound of Shadow's song ringing through the night.

Chapter Four

Consciousness returns slowly. I don't know how long it has been, but the wet dirt is cool against my cheek and a big, furry form is warm against my back. Both sensations are overwhelmed by the hunger that spears through my body. It is as sharp as my teeth and it rips into my belly like knives. A low keening noise echoes through the darkness and I realize it is mine.

The warm weight against my back rolls away and I try to push myself up from the damp ground. I manage to get onto my knees and sit back on my heels, my forehead still pressed into the dirt and my arms clutching tight around the agony in my middle.

The pain comes in waves and I breathe between them. When I open my mouth my lip splits against my teeth, which are longer and sharper than they have ever been.

Movement rustles to my side and my claws are sunk into fur before my eyes are fully open.

Everything in my head screams and I freeze.

The fur beneath my tensed fingers is black. There is no other beast in the forest with fur as black as the darkest shadow. I force my fingers to loosen my grasp by sheer will. Blood red tears roll down my face as I fight down the hunger and release my friend.

Shadow backs away, sinking to my feet and dropping a limp weight from his long muzzle. A beautiful, huge hare lays panting before me and my tears turn to sobs and I fall upon it gratefully. The first rush of blood into my mouth burns all the way down into my belly, washing away the pain.

I come back to myself minutes or hours later. The husk of the hare is cool in my hands and its life is warm in my belly. Shadow lays several feet away like a sphinx, standing guard. He stares at me for a moment and must decide I am sane again, because he rises from his post and approaches me where I kneel in the shallow ditch I dug at dawn. The hands I sink into his fur are dark with blood and dirt. The red tears I cry soak into his fur and disappear into the blackness never to be seen again.

Chapter Five

It is weeks before we venture as far as the town again. When I woke that night some of the streaks of black on my legs had not washed away with the dirt. The flesh was charred. But the next night more of the smooth white skin is revealed as the brittle black scabs slough away. Still, we stay close to my house and are comforted by its large, irregular shadow. I wish that the black, charred pieces of my home could melt away to smooth, shiny wood, but that doesn't happen.

When the moon rises, so do I. Under his watchful gaze I inspect myself. All is smooth and perfect again. No single blemish marks anywhere on my bright white skin. The evidence of my stupidity is gone, but I am determined not to forget the lesson. I might risk my own life, but I will not ever again take the chance of putting Shadow at the mercy of my hunger.

So we hunt through the night and I drink my fill, but when the sky begins to remember its colors, I am already tucked in my blackened room, fast asleep with Shadow curled by my side.

I hadn't just scared myself with my failed attempt to meet the dawn. My companion is sticking close these days, too, although I can tell the restricted range is beginning to wear on him. Finally, when he has had enough of exploring the familiar lands around my house, Shadow breaks.

I wake alone for the first time in days, and wander outside to find Shadow waiting for me in the courtyard. He bounces around like a puppy and nips at my heels in excitement.

I pretend to swat him away and Shadow plants his big paws in the dirt and drops to his elbows, tail wagging madly. His muzzle opens and his long tongue comes rolling out in an absurd grin.

I sigh. "Lead on!"

Shadow bounces away into the night and I follow on his heels, laughing at his antics. He was right—it's good to run flat out, across the big hills and through the trees. But even so, my chest tightens as we burst from their shelter and start running along the road to the town.

I slow and come to a stop at the rise of the hill, looking at the town spread out before me. Shadow bolts back and bounces up to me, tail still wagging. I frown down at him and look back toward the trees and home.

Shadow yips.

I take a step back toward the safety of the trees and Shadow sinks his teeth into the hem of my mother's dress.

"Beast!" I scold. He drops the fabric as I lunge at him and I grab it, twisting it this way and that to check for holes. Luckily for him, there is no damage. I cross my arms and glare down at the scallywag .

"You'd make a lovely coat, you know," I tell him, not at all impressed.

Unable to take a hint, the giant black wolf bounces around me like a puppy until I throw my hands up in exasperation and once again set off toward the town.

We've only made it a few streets in when I understand Shadow's eagerness. His long, sensitive snout has picked up the scent of sweet biscuits long before my own somewhat shorter version. My pace quickens and I pull in long breaths of sugary sweetness into my lungs.

Soon we are back at the walled garden and Shadow paws the ground. I shush the giant puppy and scale the wall, dropping behind a rose bush on the other side. The scent of the buttery biscuits overwhelms the garden, drowning out the musk of the roses and sharp citrus tingle of the gardenias.

As I slink up behind the bench, I can see why. The tray of biscuits is overflowing. The sweet scented heat is visible as it rises above the plate and into the air.

The girl with the silvery waves sits on the bench beside the tray once more and as I move closer she reaches out and plucks a biscuit from the top of the pile with a long sigh. I stop behind her and wait.

Several minutes pass and there is no sign of the other woman. The girl sits on the bench, occasionally pulling a biscuit from the pile.

My patience runs out and I move forward, until I am close enough to reach out and touch the cascade of silver hair. My hand brushes it as I reach forward and slide a biscuit between the slats of the bench. I take my treasure and retreat to the shadow of the rose bush, munching silently. The hair had been as soft as the silk of my mother's dresses.

I look back at the girl and she hasn't moved. I creep back up behind the bench and am preparing to take another cookie when her voice breaks the silence of the night.

"You can have as many as you'd like," she offers. Her tone is quiet but clear, like a charm that freezes me in place. My mother used to talk about the wee folk who left the fairy circles in the forest and how a tiny elf could trap a grown man with only the sound of their voice. This feels like that—like a spell. And I am caught in it.

As I sit frozen, the silver waves shift, moving to the side as the girl turns very, very slowly. The moon is no longer round in the sky and the only light in the garden comes from the house. I am in her shadow and I wonder what she can see of me.

My skin is very pale, and my eyes and hair are very dark, so I imagine she can make out my features quite easily. She can tell I am a girl, so perhaps I should act like one. I unfold myself from my feral crouch, straightening my back as my mother would have.

"Charmed, I'm sure," I tell the girl as I reach over the bench to grab the tray and spirit it away.

Laughter rings out behind me like silver bells peeling through the night.

Chapter Six

Once again I am perched at the top of the garden wall, and breathing in the heavenly scents from within. There are sugary biscuits again, and so much more. The warm vanilla of cakes, the sharp tang of lemon squares, and the ripe sweetness of berries all hang on the night air. Memories of my mother flood me. I can see her so clearly, serving these treats in our sun-filled kitchen, smiling down at me as I bite into icing and sugar.

I leap to the well-manicured lawn and stop in the shadow of my favorite rosebush to behold the wonders before me. The girl sits on a dark patterned rug laid out upon the grass, the folds of her light colored dress in a circle around her. Before her, the rug is covered from edge to edge with treats of all kinds. Colors and textures overflow trays and plates. In the center a filigreed metal stand offers up small round cakes topped in swirls of creamy frosting.

My heart skips a beat.

The girl is looking down at a book laid open across her lap, raising a hand to turn a page every now and then. I pad carefully across the grass—or I try to. My eyes are locked onto the treasures laid out before me. I don't see the dried leaf nestled between the blades of grass until it's too late. The crunch as I step down upon it is barely a sigh against the other sounds of the night but the girl's head pops up and our eyes meet.

Even in the dark, her eyes are bright. Gray or blue or green, I'm not sure, but they are light against the dark rim of her lashes. Her brows are dark, nearly black, and jarring against her pale skin and silver hair.

We both stand there frozen for a moment. The girl's eyes are wide and I hesitate, waiting for her to scream or run away. I'm ready to retreat back over the wall when she inhales, her chest expanding, and raises a thin arm to gesture across the wealth of sweets.

"Please join me for tea," she coaxes me forward.

Rising up from my crouch, I stand with a straight spine, shoulders back. I lift my skirt and bob, then approach and sink to the other end of the rug, the sweets a sugary mountain between us.

"My name is Lyssa," she tells me, but of course I know that. She looks at me expectantly and I glance down at the little round cakes, caressing their piped frosting with my eyes.

We sit there in silence for another minute and Lyssa leans forward. She lifts a little round cake from the top of the filigree stand and continues to lean forward, carrying it over the other treats, moving it toward me. Her body arches over the sweets, her arm fully extended and beginning to tremble.

"For you," she breathes unsteadily.

I'm startled from the daze I'd fallen into watching her, and accept the cake. Lyssa sinks back to her spot with a sigh, exhausted by the small effort. She watches me and I wrack my brain for a moment. Oh, yes!

"Thank you!" I say, quite proud of myself.

Lyssa's laugh rings out again, not loud but clear, like little crystals hanging in the night air. I narrow my eyes at her. Did I say something funny? Her laugh is so pretty, but if she is mocking me, I'll squish her like a bug. I slam the little round cake into my mouth and jump to my feet, ready to fly back over the wall in a huff.

"Wait! Wait!" she cries, her laughter turning to distress. "Please don't go! I'm so sorry!"

I am poised to run, my body already beginning to turn away, but the desperation in her voice tugs at me. Her emotions are like mud that slows my reactions and cools my anger. I find myself turning back to her, still standing on the rug. Her pale, thin arm is outstretched toward me and she lets it drop to her lap.

"Please stay," Lyssa says, her voice thick with tears.

I stand frozen for a moment longer and then drop back down. I am much less graceful this time and my skirts flop around me.

Lyssa's lips tremble as she smiles, tears drying on her face.

"I wasn't laughing at you, I swear," she says. Her face is so pale in the meager moonlight that it seems like a wound in the night. She has no filter or shield. Everything she feels is laid bare before me so I have no choice but to believe her.

"I was just happy." Her shoulders fall as her body seems to deflate.

I cock my head at her, confused. When Lyssa looks back up at me, I raise one eyebrow and her smile is back and bright as ever.

"I've been so lonely and I'm so happy that you're here," she explains.

"Marie?" I ask, nodding toward the house.

"How did you—You were watching?" Lyssa seems surprised.

I nod.

"Marie is lovely, but she's just here to make sure I eat," Lyssa says, which doesn't make sense. I'd seen her eat the biscuits. "And to report back to my parents, of course."

I shake my head a little, confused but not concerned enough to ask. Instead I reach out and grab one of the little cakes and extend it across to her, rising to my knees.

"For you," I offer solemnly.

Lyssa's smile is blinding as she takes it from my hand.

"Thank you," she replies, her voice warm.

The sounds of the night return as silence falls in the garden. There is the soft flutter of wings as sleeping birds shuffle in the trees and the tiny scratching of small warm things burrowing in the dry leaves. Lyssa's breath sighs between the crisp crunch of the wafer thin caramel cookie she is biting into. I am eating a berry tart and the buttery crust crumbles and I can hear each piece as it bounces onto the skirt of my dress.

Lyssa wipes the caramel residue from her fingers onto an embroidered napkin and glances at me from beneath her eyelashes. I stare back at her, fascinated by the play of emotions so visible upon her face yet so hard for me to decipher.

"Can you tell me your name?" she asks, finally.

The sound of footsteps precedes Marie's call, "Miss? It's quite late, you must come in."

Lyssa turns to watch the woman enter the garden. By the time she turns back I am already at the top of the wall. Her eyes search the darkness. I know she can't see me, but I wave anyway as I slip over the side. I have three small round cakes clutched to my chest and I immediately give one to Shadow, who waits for me.

Chapter Seven

The garden is dark and empty. No sweet scents compete with the musky roses, no matter how deeply I breathe in the night air. I sit perched atop the garden wall and gaze with disappointment at the darkness before me. The only light comes from a single window high up in the big house.

As I watch, a figure passes before the window once, then again. It's Marie, the woman who brought the sweets to Lyssa. Her face is pale and unhappy and she holds her hands clasped against her chest as if in fear.

My own chest becomes tight.

Rising to my feet on the wide edge of the stone wall, I run down its length to where the structure connects to the side of the house. The first windowsill is now within arm's reach and I pull myself up to stand upon it. The sill is made of stone and protrudes the width of my foot from the wall. It is a simple thing to leap from sill to sill until I reach the illuminated window.

Here I exercise caution. From the neighboring sill I lean out until I can see into the room, my fingers anchored into the stone casing of the window.

"I must send the letter, Miss Lyssa," Marie says as she paces.

"No," comes a faint but firm voice from the shadowed recesses of the bed. The curtains in one corner flutter and a pale hand reaches out, gesturing weakly. "There's really no point, Marie."

"You shouldn't be alone, Miss Lyssa," the woman tells her, walking back to the bed and sitting in the chair pulled up alongside it. The pale hand appears again and Marie grasps it in both of hers.

"I'm not alone, Marie. I have you and the girl in the garden to keep me company."

Even my eyes can't penetrate the dark interior of the bed but I can hear the smile in Lyssa's voice.

"Oh, Miss," Marie sighs, her voice thick with tears. She sweeps back the curtain to reveal Lyssa's pale form. "You should have more than an old maid and an imaginary friend by your side if this is..." Her voice trails off. "Let me send the letter to your parents, Miss. Maybe they'll come back in time."

"Oh, Marie. You know they won't." The girl laughs and it is sad and brittle and not at all like it had been in the garden. I hate this laugh.

I frown and lean a little further toward the window, my gaze running over the new hollows in Lyssa's face. The glow of the gas lights lining the walls must catch against my white skin because Lyssa's eyes flash to mine for a moment. Her expression doesn't change but I'm sure she's seen me.

"Help me sit up, Marie," she instructs, a new firmness in her voice. The woman jumps up to do her bidding, clucking over her like a mother hen. When Lyssa's pillows are arranged to her satisfaction Marie goes to sit back down but Lyssa grabs her hand to stop her. "Do we have any of the lemon biscuits left in the kitchen?"

Marie gasps and clasps her hands together as if the girl has given her a gift.

"I don't think so, Miss," she tells her, "But I'll whip some up! It won't take me long at all." Marie bustles out the door, looking much happier than she had a moment ago.

Lyssa's eyes track Marie's departure and then swing back to the window.

I lean forward and a smile lights up her face, returning a touch of color to her cheeks.

In one fluid motion I leap through the open window and land lightly upon the carpet into a low curtsy. I rise from my graceful bow, an answering smile stretching across my mouth.

Lyssa freezes and her new color leaches from her face. She is even paler than before, something I wouldn't have thought possible. Living things aren't usually that color. Besides me, of course.

"Are you dying?" I rear back and then move forward again, cocking my head at her. I realize I am quite concerned and would be very disappointed if that was the case.

Lyssa startles at my question and bursts into surprised laughter. She holds a hand over her stomach as she chuckles weakly until clear tears leak from her eyes.

"Well, yes," she says once she has herself back under control.

Chapter Eight

I lounge in the cozy spot beneath Lyssa's bed as Marie moves around the room. She fusses at the girl, excited by her consumption of a single lemon biscuit and a glass of water. The sweet, sharp scent of the biscuits calls to me and I am eager for Marie to bustle herself right back out of the room.

"I'm feeling much better, Marie," Lyssa tells her, "But I am very tired. I'm going to try to sleep now."

"I'll grab my darning, Miss, and just keep you company–"

"Oh, no!" Lyssa interrupts her. "It's so late, you should just go to bed."

"I've gotten used to staying up nights with you, Miss." Marie doesn't sound particularly put out by this and Lyssa chuckles.

"We've become quite the night owls, haven't we?" she asks.

The two laugh at each other and I consider jumping out from under the bed to remind Lyssa that I'm here. Perhaps she senses the impending limit to my patience and begins to move the conversation along.

"I'll be quite all right, Marie," she says softly but firmly. "You go on to bed. I promise I'll be here in the morning."

After a moment of silence, Marie's footsteps tap toward the door. They hesitate for a moment.

"Oh, no, please leave the lights, Marie."

"Of course, Miss. Sleep well."

"Thank you, Marie. For everything."

The door closes with a soft click and I am out from under the bed in a heartbeat.

"Who bit you?" I blurt out. Who has thought to hurt this girl who is so generous with her wonderful, sugary treasures? She doesn't answer but holds one of the biscuits out to me, luring me to her side.

"There's been no biting," she responds finally, once I've taken the biscuit.

My instinct is to retreat back to the window, but I stay beside her bed. She is still sitting up on her mountain of fluffed pillows, and the bed is tall, so our heads are nearly at the same level. The gas lights cast a yellow glow over everything in the room, turning Lyssa's hair to gold.

"Sometimes I bite," I tell her, and demonstrate with my sweet lemon biscuit.

Lyssa's eyes drop to my sharp teeth and widen the smallest amount. "I see that."

I swallow the piece of biscuit in my mouth before answering, as my mother taught me. "Not just biscuits," I confess.

"Are you going to bite me?" she asks, her voice calm and low.

"No," I assure her. "I don't bite people." And then I ruin it. "Usually." I turn back to the window and step up to the sill.

"Wait!" she cries out, leaning forward in the bed. "You never told me your name."

I pause, perched on her windowsill and turn back to her, meeting her gaze. "You won't die tonight, will you?"

"Will you come back tomorrow?" she asks, her voice strained.

I nod.

"Then no, I won't die tonight." Lyssa sighs as she sags back against her pillows.

"My name is Sharptooth," I whisper and slip out into the night.

Shadow is terribly disappointed in me when I return to his side empty handed. For the rest of the evening I pick nettles out of his coat and paws in contrition. When we lie curled up in my room at sunrise, his rough tongue scrapes my hand in acceptance of my apology.

He is still by my side when I wake many hours later and I run my hands through his fur for a moment, not quite ready to greet the night.

Eventually, though, nature calls him out of the house. Shadow has learned I get very, very cross at wet spots in my room. Once he waters the tall grasses that have grown up around the blackened front stairs, we set out into the forest.

The moon is still struggling out from its shadow and there are many dark spots hiding small warm things among the trees. I know I could sit and wait and they would come to me, but that isn't my mood this evening. I fly over the forest floor, my long black hair absorbing the meager light and forming a deep well of blackness in my wake. I am a dark comet shooting through the sky, my trail made up of shadow instead of fire.

Then I am crashing to the earth, tangled in someone else's furred limbs and claws. Close by, Shadow is yipping but I stay focused on the teeth snapping at my face. A light colored muzzle comes at me again and again and I hold it away, my own claws clutching the beast's neck.

This creature is not a small warm thing. It is large and gives off heat like a flame. Its fur has a golden cast in the moonlight and its teeth are just as long as mine.

But mine are sharper.

The beast's fur is thick and its skin tough, but my teeth and claws sink deep and soon my hands are covered in its blood. We roll across the forest floor, my back hitting the rough bark of a tree, clods of dirt flying in our wake. Over its shoulder black flashes as Shadow lunges for one of the flailing limbs and misses.

I still have both hands around the creature's neck and I push it back as far as I can. It snaps at my face but its muzzle is much shorter and rounder than my friend's and it cannot reach me with its teeth.

Its legs, however, are long.

I am dimly aware of claws raking across my belly and down my legs, but none of that matters. I keep squeezing. Tighter and tighter as my own claws dig into the cat's neck—for that's what it is—and its movements slow until finally it hangs limp in my grasp.

My panting breath sends needles of pain through my entire body as I stand in the forest, holding the beast before me by the neck. The tips of its front legs dangle in the short grass of the forest floor and its rump and back legs rest upon the ground.

Its body from shoulder to hip is longer than mine from head to toe. I've never seen a predator this large in the forest.

Shadow raises a paw and knocks at the huge cat and I let it fall to the ground. In an instant, we both descend upon it.

Chapter Nine

I perch on the wall, the garden deserted below me. I don't breathe easily again until I've made my way to the lone lit window where the girl is sitting up in the bed, a book in her hand and a plate of small cakes beside her.

She is alone in the room so I swing through the open window and land lightly on the carpeted floor. Lyssa looks up at me and gasps.

"You're hurt!" she cries.

I looked down at myself in confusion. The skin visible through the tears in my dress is smooth, but stained with blood, only some of which is mine.

"You *were* hurt," Lyssa says slowly.

I shrug and she rolls her eyes at me. Lyssa leans forward and gestures for me to come closer.

My feet drag as I approach the bed and I take in every detail of Lyssa's appearance. The arm she stretches toward me is bird-like, every bone visible in her hand and wrist. When I am close enough she plucks at the torn edges of my dress and her skin is as pale as mine, nearly white in the dim light from the gas lanterns.

"Something attacked you," she insists.

"Cat," I shrug.

Lyssa's tinkling laugh rings out and a weight lifts from my chest that I hadn't been aware of until it was gone. I smile and her focus shifts to my mouth and her eyes widen. I refuse to hide my teeth.

"It must have been a very *big* cat," she ponders.

I nod, because it was, and my gaze moves to the plate of pretty pink-iced cakes now within my reach.

"You didn't have these last night," she points out, gesturing to the tears in my dress. "This happened today?"

I nod again, my brow furrowed as I try to figure out the reasons behind her questions. The sugar and vanilla sweetness of the tiny cakes, each one decorated with a perfect rose made of icing, distracts me.

Lyssa finally takes pity on me.

"Please take one," she sighs. "I only ever really request the sweets for you, you know."

I pluck a cake from the tray and pop the entire thing into my mouth as I consider her words.

Once I can speak again, I ask very carefully, "You don't like sweets?"

The girl scoffs. "I'm not crazy, I swear! I do like sweets." Her voice becomes more serious and the smile falls from her face. "I don't eat very much these days."

I pluck another cake from the tray and stand before her, waiting for her to continue. I eat this cake more slowly. I am, after all, quite full of cat.

Lyssa slumps back against her pillows and sighs.

"I'm quite sick, you see," she confesses. "There's nothing the doctor can do about it and everyone seems to be resigned to the inevitability of my impending death."

There is no blood, no wounds on her head or arms. I grasp the thick quilted bed covering and fling it off her to reveal her injuries. There is nothing. Her frilly white nightgown stops at her little round knees. While her legs are pale and thin like her arms, they have no obvious defects.

My eyes sweep up and down her body, seeing nothing to support her claim. Focusing on her face again, I find her eyes large and round and her mouth hanging open like a fish.

"Where?" I demand. I need her to show me the problem so that I can fix it.

It takes the girl a moment to compose herself. She pushes up off the pillows and pulls her legs in to sit with them folded before her and drapes her nightgown over them. Sitting forward like this, we are even closer, the tall bed putting her at nearly my height. She takes a little pink cake from the tray and looks down at it in her hands.

"I'm not sure how to explain it," she starts. "There's something wrong inside. An imbalance of the humors, the doctor said. The bile and the blood—"

"Blood?" Finally, something that makes sense. "It hurts? Inside?" I gesture at my own belly.

"Yes," Lyssa confirms. "It makes it hard to eat and hard to sleep. The pain is so sharp."

I nod, understanding. This is a problem I know how to fix.

Chapter Ten

"Absolutely not," the girl announces.

I look down at the offering in my hands, not seeing the cause of her consternation. It is a lovely hare, fat and furry and still quite warm.

"Bite it," I repeat.

Her dark eyebrows drop and her lips flatten. "No," she says firmly.

"Why?" I ask in confusion. It is a very fine thing that I have caught for her. I am quite proud of it as I hold it by its ears, its bright red blood dripping onto the carpet by Lyssa's bed.

"Oh, please," she cries, "take it away!"

A door slams from somewhere in the house and we both turn toward the sound. By the time the door opens to admit Marie, the hare and I are tucked out of sight under the tall bed. I meet its flat, dead eyes and shrug.

"Miss, are you in pain?" Marie asks. "I heard you cry out."

There is shuffling from the bed and Lyssa answers, her voice tight. "I'm fine, Marie. Please go back to bed."

Footsteps retreat toward the door and then stop. There is a moment of silence and a gasp from surprisingly close by. I tense, preparing for an attack.

"Oh, Miss! Is this blood?" There are tears in the woman's voice.

"It's not mine!" Lyssa tells her, exasperation creeping back into her voice. "My friend brought me a gift."

"Oh, Miss," Marie cries. She fusses over Lyssa for several minutes more, ignoring the girl's attempts at deflection. I consider revealing myself, or perhaps pushing the hare out from under the bed to explain the blood on the carpet, but the memory of Lyssa's lowered eyebrows stays my hand .

Finally, Marie hurries out of the room. I climb out from under the bed as the girl flops back on her pillows and throws a hand over her eyes.

"Out," she says, pointing to the window.

I am perched on the sill, the hare still dangling from my hand, when she calls out again, "But please come back tomorrow! I don't mean to be ungrateful."

She stares after me earnestly and I nod, slipping out into the night.

Landing on the other side of the garden wall, I toss the hare to Shadow. He'd been quite put out when I'd taken it with me and his eyes are alight at its return. Within minutes the entire carcass is gone and he smiles at me, tongue hanging from his open mouth in glee.

At least one of my friends is happy.

Some nights Shadow's family accompanies us on our run through the forest. It took the mother wolf a very long time to let me near her babies, but now I think perhaps she has decided that I am one of them. She nudges my hip as we run side by side and when we stop to eat our fill, she lets me rub her large, firm, pointed ears and sink my fingers into the thick hair around her neck.

Our bellies full and warm, she sits at my side, touching, while Shadow and her other children sprawl across the grass around us. My fingers run through her hair as she cleans a spot on my leg, but my thoughts are in the town house.

When the sharp pains stabbed into my stomach it did feel like I was dying. I don't want the girl, Lyssa, to feel that. Her face is tired and sad when she talks about dying. I'm tired and sad when I think about her dying. I'm also angry...and afraid.

The anger is better, I decide.

Later that night, as I look up at the smiling moon, I gather my anger to me before I climb the wall to the garden. It pushes the sadness and fear out of the way, and I slip into Lyssa's window determined to make her see reason.

She sits on the tall bed, leaning against her mountain of pillows with her hands clasped before her and her face pale and tight. On the table beside her bed sits a tray of tiny little swirls made of pastry. The scent of their fruity filling overwhelms the room.

"You can't come tomorrow night," she says, the moment she sees me.

I nearly stagger at the bolt of pain that shoots through me at her words. My first instinct is to turn around and climb right back out of the window. I want to find a dark corner of the forest to hide from the hurt of her words.

"It isn't safe," she continues, pausing my internal spiral.

"Safe?" I ask, still frozen by the window.

"My parents are on their way. It won't be safe for you to be here."

"Is it safe for you?"

Lyssa's laugh is sad, the one that I hate. "What could they possibly do to me?"

Sitting up, Lyssa folds her legs under the covers and sets the tray of pastry swirls before her on the bed. "These are fig," she says as I crawl onto the bed across from her.

I cross my legs and lean forward to pluck a treat from the tray between us. The buttery pastry melts against my tongue and the fruit filling buzzes with flavor. I take my time chewing and gather my thoughts.

"I like sweets," I start.

Lyssa's laugh cuts me off. It is a small, quiet laugh, but it is her real laugh, not the sad one. "I noticed," she mocks me.

I wrinkle my nose at her. "But," I continue firmly, "they are not enough. They fill my belly but I'm still hungry. Still hurt."

"Hurt?" she asks, tiling her head.

"Sweets don't fix things," I explain, gesturing to the rips across the bodice of my mother's black dress.

"How did you heal your wounds then?" Lyssa's eyes take in the unmarked skin revealed by the shredded cotton.

"Blood." The answer seems so obvious to me.

"That won't work for me!" Lyssa seems appalled by the idea, pressing her hand to her chest.

"Why not?" She doesn't know the warm, sweet rush of blood, coursing down your throat and soothing the sharp pains throughout your body.

"I don't—I can't," Lyssa stutters, flailing as she tries to explain her reservations. "I can't take blood from a creature without consent," she finally settles on.

I raise my eyebrows. "That seems...unlikely."

Lyssa scoffs at me. "You know what I mean!" She lifts a tiny pastry from the tray and uses it to wave away my skepticism before taking a dainty bite.

I snatch a pastry from the tray and pop it into my mouth, chewing aggressively.

"Your real name can't possibly be Sharptooth," Lyssa announces.

I continued to chew, ignoring her.

Lyssa gives a long suffering sigh and picks up another pastry. "What does your mother call you?"

The pastry is a rock scraping down the lining of my throat.

"My darling girl," I say finally, on a sigh. Struck by memories of soft hands and sweet smiles, I pull my knees up to my chest and wrap my arms around them, holding on tight.

Lyssa lets her hands rest in her lap, her face still.

"Where is your mother now?" she asks carefully.

I shake my head. What could I say? That she ran away? Something worse? I didn't know and it hurt to wonder.

"My mother just calls me Lyssa," she admits. "If she even talks to me at all."

I cock my head at her.

"They're not very nice, my parents," she says, her voice soft and sad.

"I'm not sure exactly what would happen if they knew you were real. Marie is convinced you're a figment of my imagination." She smiles at that.

I rather like being a figment of Lyssa's imagination, and I smile back. "I'm not worried," I tell her.

"I see that," she replies.

Chapter Eleven

The forest floor flies by under my feet as I race toward the town. I stop once to scoop up a fat little bunny, too slow to get out of my way. I leave his husk at the tree line as I turn to follow the main road.

Shadow runs beside me for most of the way but as we approach the last hill, the distant howl of his brothers and sisters calls him back to the forest. I carry on alone and soon am outside of Lyssa's house.

Every window in the house is ablaze with light and when I scale the wall, the garden is awash in firelight from several braziers dotted among the roses. I pull myself into the branches of a large tree to take in the spectacle.

Tall men in black coats and women in colorful dresses with hair piled high on their heads nod and gesture with glasses of sparkling liquid. They twitter like a flock of birds, fluttering around each other.

Glancing from face to face, I try to figure out who among the throng might be Lyssa's parents. The men all look the same in their identical suits. The women wear a rainbow of colors but their faces are all quite similarly painted, with powdered cheeks and blood red lips.

After a while, I settle upon one woman who seems to be quite important. She has light hair and dark eyebrows, like Lyssa. The man by her side looks like all of the others but his voice is a bit louder and his gestures a bit broader. They are both obviously having a very good time.

As the night wears on, many of the men and women begin to take their leave. Carriages come again and again and take them away to wherever they came from. Finally, a small group departs all at once, leaving only the light-haired woman, her male counterpart, and another man.

"Well done, Dear. Well done," the loud man tells the woman, offering her his arm. "If we had to come back to this dreary little backwater, at least I'll make some money from it." His laugh is echoed by the other man as they walk into the brightly lit interior of the house.

I drop from the shadows of the tree onto the top of the garden wall and run to the house. The lights from the windows shine like beacons into the night and I know to exercise caution when crossing them. When I make it to the window beside Lyssa's, I lean out to gaze into the girl's room.

The three figures from the party walk through the door, startling Marie, who jumps up from the chair by Lyssa's bed. The woman who must be Lyssa's mother crosses to stand at the foot of the bed.

"How is she, Marie?" she asks, her painted lips red as fresh blood against her pale powdered cheeks.

"I'm fine, Mother," Lyssa responds forcefully.

Lyssa's mother continues to look toward Marie, who glances between the two in discomfort.

"Lyssa is feeling better this evening, Ma'am," Marie finally speaks. "I've even gotten her to eat some of these iced gingersnaps." Marie gestures to the tray on Lyssa's bedside table.

"Thank you, Marie." Lyssa's mother waves a hand dismissively.

Glancing nervously toward the pale girl in the bed, Marie nods and lowers her head as she passes the men still standing by the doorway and ducks from the room.

I now have an unobstructed view of Lyssa, lying in her bed. She looks small. Her face is pale and tight, her lips pressed together in a straight line.

Would I be angry like this if my mother came back for me? If she could.

"I am fine, Mother," Lyssa bites out each word as if she's ripping it off the bone.

"This is Lord Mannix, your father's new business partner," her mother announces with a wave of her hand toward the quieter of the two men. "And your betrothed." She claps her hands in glee.

I'm frozen in confusion, but Lyssa snaps back, "You must be insane." Color rushes into her pale face and her hands clench at the bed linens.

"Oh, come now!" exclaims the loud man, who must be Lyssa's father. "This is a fabulous match. With Lord Mannix's partnership the company will be able to expand to the eastern trade routes!" He gives a robust pat to the back of the man beside him, who does not flinch under the blow. Lord Mannix, who is somewhat taller and thinner than Lyssa's father, gives a small close-lipped smile in return, his eyes assessing everyone in the room.

"What does that have to do with me?" Lyssa demands. "I'm barely thirteen. You can't possibly be serious." Her voice is strained, the anger edging into desperation.

My fingers bite into the stone frame of the window sill as I hold myself back from flying through the opening and launching myself at these interlopers.

When Lyssa told me that her parents were coming, I'd had the urge to grab her hand and pull her into the forest. I imagined that they would gather her into their arms and she would disappear into their embrace. And I would be alone again. My heart was braced for the pain of losing her.

But there would be no loving embrace from these people. I remember my mother being sad and afraid but I don't remember her ever speaking to me the way that

Lyssa's parents speak to her. My mother held my hand, her arm around me–even when I bit her. My mother always touched me with love.

Lyssa's parents don't touch her. They don't even look at her.

Mannix, the tall man, approaches the bed where Lyssa is lying and she cringes back against her pillows. A piece of the stone window casing breaks off beneath my lengthening claws, but I hold my position, outside the path of light from the window. The man leans over Lyssa and rakes his eyes down her length.

"Just hold on long enough to get through the wedding, girl," he tells her in a voice devoid of any emotion.

"And the wedding night!" her father adds, cackling.

Beside him, Lyssa's mother claps her hands. "Let us retire to the study for a nightcap, gentlemen. It has been a long day." She waves toward the door and ushers the men from the room.

"And a productive one!" Lyssa's father chortles as he leads the way.

Mannix hesitates at the doorway, looking back toward Lyssa as she lies in the bed, clutching the coverlet to her chest.

"Indeed," he adds, before sweeping from the room.

Lyssa's mother follows them without looking back at her daughter, closing the door behind her with a click.

Between one heartbeat and the next I am through the window. Like a shadow I fly across the room and onto the bed. Lyssa's eyes are wide, white showing all the way around the edges. She releases the cover and reaches for me, sinking her thin, pale fingers into the torn bodice of my dress. I wrap her in my arms as her thin shoulders begin to shake. We stay like that for a long time, the only sound in the room her sobs muffled against my neck.

Chapter Twelve

Lyssa and I sit on her bed, planning our escape. Or arguing. I'm planning our escape, and Lyssa is arguing.

"I can barely walk, Sharptooth! How would I even get out of this room, much less out of town and into the forest?" she scoffs. "It's just not possible."

"I will bring you a hare and you will bite it." I repeat calmly. We've been over this several times. "The pain will go away. You will be strong and we will run together through the night." I look her firmly in the eye and hold onto her hand. "It will be wonderful."

Lyssa pulls her hand from mine and throws both of hers into the air. She laughs a sad, brittle laugh.

"I wish it were that simple." She shakes her head, tears back in her eyes.

I lean forward to catch her gaze again. "It is."

"My teeth aren't like yours," she whines. "Look at them!" Lyssa bares her square teeth at me and she is right. They are not like mine and they would make it difficult to bite a hare.

She has teeth for sweets, not small warm things.

Grabbing an iced gingersnap from the bedside table, I bite my finger and a bead of bright red blood wells up on its tip. Holding it over the gingersnap, I let a single drop fall upon the soft white icing and sink into its surface. The blood disappears, leaving behind a pink dot.

I nod at my handiwork and offer it to Lyssa. She examines the icing for a long moment, finally shrugging her shoulders and popping the entire thing into her mouth. Eyes shut tight, she begins to chew. As her jaw works, her expression clears and she opens her eyes. Her throat works as she swallows the doctored treat.

"Well, that wasn't too bad," she confesses.

I grab another gingersnap from the tray to repeat the process. The wound on my finger has already closed so I bite it again and startle when Lyssa grabs my hand. She stares at the small hole that my teeth have made in the pad at the end of my finger. We both watch as blood wells up from the wound, then recedes as the hole closes.

"Fascinating," Lyssa whispers as she rubs her own soft finger across the now unblemished skin.

I reclaim my finger and bite it again, focusing on the task before me as I drip blood onto the next gingersnap.

This time there is no argument and Lyssa eats cookie after cookie decorated with pink dots of me.

"No more," she announces and slumps back against her mountain of pillows, smiling. Her legs are no longer tucked under the thick blankets and there is a touch of color in her cheeks.

I am quite pleased.

"You feel better," I say, not a question. Lyssa is more relaxed than I've ever seen her.

"I do," she admits. "My body feels warm and heavy. I feel as if I'm full for the first time in my entire life." Lyssa pauses, head cocked. "Nothing hurts."

Multiple expressions cascade across Lyssa's face, but the one I recognize is fear. I remember seeing the same look on my mother's face.

"I won't bite you," I rush to assure her.

Lyssa shakes her head. "I know." But her eyes are still wide.

"Don't be afraid of me," I beg her. My own eyes sting with tears and I take in a deep breath to hold them back. I know the sight of my red tears would only make things worse.

"I'm not," Lyssa insists, her fear being pushed out by irritation. "I've never been afraid of you, and I'm not going to start now."

"You looked afraid," I point out, my panic beginning to recede.

"I am concerned," Lyssa enunciates, drawing the word out. "And I have every right to be," she continues, her little nose rising.

I sit there, waiting for her to explain. The girl huffs as If she was waiting for me to ask a question, but I have no idea where to start.

Giving a long-suffering sigh, Lyssa finally continues. "This isn't normal, you know. I've read every book in this house and there are several on medicine and anatomy and this is *not* how things work."

"It *is* working," I point out.

"Well, something is happening," Lyssa admits. "I just need to figure out what."

"You're getting better," I tell her. "You'll see."

When I leave Lyssa's room, the lights still blaze in the big house and I am very careful as I pass each window. Laughter echoes from the last window, so I slow and take a peek around the casing. Lyssa's parents are lounging upon overstuffed couches while Mannix leans against a large ornate fireplace.

I am tempted to bolt across the opening but the tall man is facing the window and seems much more alert than his companions. His eyes flick in my direction and I move out of sight.

Weighing the distance to the end of the building against the wrapped bundle of gingersnaps currently occupying my hands, I leap lightly down to the ground and make my way between the rose bushes. At the end of the garden I scale the wall one-handed and find Shadow waiting for me in the grass on the other side.

He follows me—or the gingersnaps—through the town and over the fields until we finally collapse in the fairy circle. I toss gingersnaps at the beast and he wiggles in the grass on his back, four huge clawed feet waving in the air. My laughter rings out through the trees.

When we finally make our way back to the black husk of my home, Shadow follows me to my room and snuggles against my side on the cold, hard floor. I sink my fingers into his fur as the morning pulls me into sleep. My last thought is of sitting in Lyssa's big, soft bed, her finger brushing over mine as she searches for a scar that isn't there.

Chapter Thirteen

I wake up thinking of Lyssa's mother. After sending Shadow outside to take care of business, I wander the house, eventually walking into my mother's bedroom.

Beneath the black char coating every surface there are memories waiting to be discovered. Each of the dresses in the large wardrobe sparks visions of walks in the sunlight, carriage rides, and visits with strangers. Beneath the soot and dust on the dresser, a tarnished mirror brings a sharp vision of my mother brushing my hair.

I sift through the debris to find the beautiful carved handle brush from my memory. Holding the brush awkwardly, I try to swipe at the wild ends of my long black hair. I remember my mother taking long sweeps of the brush from the top of my head to the ends, but the bristles snag and pull and I soon give up.

Going back to the dresses, I shuffle past the bright colors to find a deep, dark blue hiding in the back. Pulling the dress from the wardrobe I hold it before me. I don't remember my mother ever wearing this dress. It is much plainer than the others, the style a simple pleated panel from neck to ribs and then a straight fall to the ground.

I use my claws to rip away what is left of the black dress and let it fall to the floor of my mother's room. The big cat left it in tatters and running through the trees every night has not improved its condition. The blue dress is almost as dark—the color of the sky around the full moon.

It is also much easier to get into. I simply hold it over my head and pull the fitted part down to my ribs and I am done. No laces or hooks or buttons to fuss with or leave gaping. I love it. I spin this way and that and the skirt floats around my legs like a cloud.

Tucking the brush into the top of my dress, I fly from the house. Shadow is lounging with a fresh carcass in the middle of the drive, his face a happy mess. I laugh at him and set out to find my own breakfast.

When my belly is full and warm, I make my way to Lyssa's house. Shadow catches an interesting scent at the edge of the town and bounds off, his dark fur lost to the night. Alone, I continue on.

Once again the house is ablaze with light. Every window glows yellow from the gas lanterns inside and I take a moment to admire the lights. There are other houses with gas lanterns, but none have so many or use them so recklessly.

Circling to the garden, I find it occupied. Lyssa's parents and Lord Mannix sit around an ornate wood table, surrounded by metal braziers giving off heat and light. The three laugh and gesture, the table before them strewn with the remains of their meal.

"Lemons into lemonade, I always say," announces Lyssa's father, knocking on the top of the table.

"Well, I think your little lemon is something of a peach and I'm happy to help," replies the other man, raising his glass.

The father shakes his head. "Nothing but trouble, my good man. Nothing but trouble since the moment Estelle popped the chit out."

Lyssa's mother cackles. "Popped? I wish it would have been that easy. Three days and three nights! And that sickly little smart-mouthed beast is all I have to show for it."

"It's true," her husband agrees. "A less grateful girl you'd be hard-pressed to find. It will be a blessedly short engagement, Mannix."

"And an even shorter marriage, no doubt," his wife scoffs.

Mannix swirls the liquid in his glass, gazing at the contents. "We'll see. We'll see."

"Either way, I'm happy to cement our partnership," the father booms, holding his glass aloft. "To the future!"

The other two clink their glasses against his and all three drink.

I drop down from the garden wall and make my way around the outside of the house, every step filled with rage and frustration. How dare they speak about Lyssa in such a manner? How dare they *give* her to this horrible man who seems to be full of nothing but bad intentions?

Rounding the corner of the stone building, I spot movement from a side door and duck back out of sight. The moon is still a sliver in the sky but the light cast from the house illuminates the surrounding area. Marie and another woman carry large basins of water from the house. They walk them across the alley beside the house and began dumping them into the drain built into the edge of the cobbled street.

"It seems a bit of a disgrace," the unknown woman says, "such a young girl marrying."

"I know," Marie responds. "My poor poppet." She shakes her head. "I feel quite responsible, you know. I sent them a letter that we were getting close to the end. I know they've never been what one might call *warm* parents...but I thought they'd at least want to say goodbye."

Finished with her task, Marie turns to look up at the stone wall of the house.

"Miss Lyssa has spent almost all of her life confined to this house and those people have barely stopped by to see her. So many birthdays and holidays spent alone.

And now, when she's approaching her end, they spring this on her."

"At least it is a very good match," the other woman points out. "Lord Mannix has a comfortable living and a lovely estate."

"I doubt that poor girl will get to see any of it..."

The women disappear into the house and I run up to the door on silent feet. After listening for a moment, I try the handle. The door swings open and I step into a memory.

Chapter Fourteen

This is what my house used to look like. The walls are smooth and light, no blackened char or soot anywhere. The floors are clean and smooth. I float through the doorway and down the hall in a daze of memories. The hallway before me has a railing halfway up with raised wood panels below and a textured wallpaper above, but I am seeing gray stripes and thick white moldings.

In my house there are three doors leading from the hallway, each one a bedroom. The first open doorway reveals a small sitting room and I am startled from my fog. This is not my house. This is Lyssa's house and her bedroom is on the floor above.

I run down the hall and turn the corner. A large staircase curls up, wood railing gleaming in the light of the gas lanterns on each wall. All is quiet, so I dart up the stairs, trying to match the interior of the house with the view from the garden. Correlating rooms to windows, I identify Lyssa's door and stand before it, ear pressed to the wood for a moment before entering.

"Marie?" calls out Lyssa's voice from the bed, and I can breathe again.

I close the door behind me with a soft click and Lyssa leans forward, peering around the curtains. Her eyes become round white saucers in the shadowed interior of the bed when she sees me.

I allow a toothy smile to overtake my face and her eyes widen a bit more.

Launching toward the bed, I sail through the curtains and tackle her back against the pillows. Lyssa lets out a squeak that turns to giggles as I nestle in against her side. She wiggles down in the bed and turns on her side to face me, her smile as wide as mine–although less sharp.

"Oh, my dear heaven!" she whisper-screams. "I think you just gave me a heart attack."

I cock my head to the side, listening. "Nope. Sounds fine."

Lyssa rolls her eyes at me and then her face turns serious. "Can you really hear my heartbeat?" she asks, our faces close together.

I give a small nod.

Lyssa closes her eyes, frowning in concentration. Her face is still pale against the snow white of her lacy pillow sham, but now there is pink in her cheeks and her lips are a soft rose. The dark shadows around her eyes are lighter and she looks more rested than I've ever seen her.

Her eyes snap open, long dark lashes sweeping up. "I hear it!" she announces. "And I can hear yours too. That's amazing!"

"You couldn't hear it before?" I know she has had difficulty walking and has spent a lot of her time sitting and lying in bed. Actually, I realize, I've never seen Lyssa standing.

Without waiting for her response, I crawl over her and climb from the bed to stand beside it. I grab Lyssa's hand and tug.

"Up," I demand. I can't wait to see her standing.

Lyssa resists my pull for a moment and then gives a little sigh. She sweeps the bed covers back, and scoots forward to the edge of the bed. I step back to give her room and use my grip on her hand to pull her onto her feet.

And just like that Lyssa and I are standing nose to nose. Or maybe nose to eyeball. Lyssa's dark winged brow sits at my eye line and I look down to meet her gaze. This close, Lyssa's eyes aren't just gray. There are lines of green and blue and gold all running toward the black at the center. Her lashes are starkly black against her skin as she lowers her gaze, so much darker than her silvery hair.

"You're wearing a new dress," she exclaims.

I take a half step back and look down at myself, having forgotten. "Oh, yes. It's very comfortable."

"And not all ripped up," she points out. Lyssa reaches out to touch the fabric. "This material is so lovely."

"I think it was my mother's," I tell her, watching her pale hand move against the midnight blue fabric at my waist.

"It's an empire style, so more likely your grandmother's," Lyssa notes. "This dress is very old but the workmanship is amazing. And the color is gorgeous."

"I love it," I tell her.

"I do too," she looks up at me again, smiling.

Chapter Fifteen

"Come outside with me," I demand, watching Lyssa's face in the mirror above the vanity.

Lyssa's smile dims. "It's the middle of the night," she protests, continuing to brush my hair in low strokes.

Standing, I ignore her answer and tug on her hand.

"I'm wearing my night clothes," she exclaims as she digs in her heels. "I can't go outside in this. Besides, I'm sure my parents are still up with their guest and we'd be caught."

I sigh in disappointment but I know she has a point.

"Here, hide in the wardrobe and I'll ring Marie for some sweets." Lyssa walks to the large closet opposite her bed and opens the door to reveal an array of colorful dresses. I climb up into the cabinet and slip beneath them and she smiles at me. "It's just for a moment," she promises, closing the door gently.

Cocooned in darkness, I curl up on the wood floor of the wardrobe as Lyssa rings her bell and settles herself back in her bed. A moment later footsteps approach the door and Marie announces herself.

"I'm so sorry to bother you so late Marie, but as you can see I'm wide awake. Are there any of the candied plums left from earlier? Or perhaps some biscuits?" Lyssa asks.

"Of course, Miss. It's no bother at all." Marie approaches the bed and I tense. "You seem a bit flushed, Miss." There is a pause and Marie continues, "Well, your temperature seems fine." Her footsteps move back toward the door and I relax. "I'll be right back, Miss."

More soft footsteps and Lyssa's face appears among the dresses above me.

"Can you stay in there a little while longer?" she whispers, her brow furrowed.

"It's nice in here," I tell her.

She rolls her eyes and gives a little huff of a laugh. "Just a moment more," she says, shaking her head, leaving me in the soft darkness again.

Marie is back quickly, and she must have brought a feast with her. The calming scent of Lyssa's dresses is swamped by the smell of sugar and sweet fruit and something much richer. As soon as the woman bustles back out of the room I push open the door to my hiding spot to see what she's brought us.

Lyssa sits cross-legged on the bed with a large platter before her. One half is covered in sweets and the other has succulent strips of beef and chicken.

"Leftovers from my parent's dinner," Lyssa explains while saliva rushes to my mouth. "She's trying to get me to eat more meat to build my strength."

"She's right," I say, climbing back onto the bed and mirroring Lyssa's pose on the other side of the tray. I reach forward and lift a long, juicy strip of beef from the tray. It is seared on one side but the interior is still a lovely pink and translucent red drops splash onto the tray. I bite the end off of the strip and nearly groan out loud with approval.

Watching me, Lyssa selects the smallest piece of beef and picks it up with two fingers. She leans over the plate to take the tiniest nibble and sits back, chewing thoughtfully.

"It is quite good," she admits.

We dig into our feast, making use of the linen napkins Marie has left to clean up our fingers and faces. When there are only three small sweets left on the tray, I bite my finger and hover it over each one until my blood seeps into the sugar toppings.

"That really should be quite off-putting," Lyssa muses.

"But it isn't?"

"No." She seems surprised by her own admission. "In fact," she begins with both wonder and concern in her voice, "it is rather enticing."

I hold out the treat and Lyssa takes it carefully, slowly raising it to her lips. She pops the treat into her mouth and chews it before swallowing.

"Good?" I ask.

"Yes."

Chapter Sixteen

Lyssa's parents continue to use the garden for their entertaining nearly every evening. Sometimes they host dozens of brightly dressed women and black-suited men and sometimes it is only Lord Mannix who joins them. I try to listen to their conversations but for the most part they talk about nothing. They only ever speak about Lyssa in reference to her upcoming marriage to Lord Mannix.

I become quite adept at sneaking into the house and exploring its hallways. Despite the lack of soot and char, it is actually quite similar to my own home. The kitchen is the lowest level, the lounges and libraries above, and the bedrooms at the top.

The longer Lyssa's parents stay in residence, the more help Marie has in the house. There are now two other women and a dour-faced man walking its halls at all hours of the night and the lights blaze continuously. It becomes quite a game to avoid detection as I explore the house.

After a close call, I slip into Lyssa's room to find her standing before the open wardrobe. She has a rich brown dress hanging from her shoulders, the back gaping open to expose the long line of her smooth white skin.

She turns when I step into the room, a hand coming to her chest when she recognizes me.

"Oh, I thought you were Marie for a moment," Lyssa gasps. "I don't want to have to explain why I'm dressing."

"Why are you dressing?" I ask with a smile.

"I am ready for a walk," she announces, eyes twinkling. "Can you help me with the buttons on the back?"

Lyssa turns back to the wardrobe. Most of her silvery hair is pulled up into an elaborate pile on the top of her head, but the back cascades down and over one shoulder. I step up close behind her, examining the tiny closures running down the back of the dress. Starting at her waist, I slip each little bone button into the corresponding loop, the backs of my fingers brushing against her warm skin. Lyssa reaches back a hand to sweep the hair from her neck, exposing the last button.

"Done," I announce, stepping back.

Lyssa spins back toward me and I examine her face. Her skin is still pale, but her cheeks and the tip of her nose are dusted with pink. Her lips are a rich rose.

Lyssa's pale gray eyes are bright under her dark brows and even her silvery hair seems shinier and thicker.

"You feel better."

Lyssa smiles widely. "I do."

We arrange the pillows on Lyssa's bed into a roughly body-shaped mass under the blankets, pull the curtains at the four corners to cast the interior in deep shadow, and douse all but one of the lights. Lyssa leads me to the servant's stairs, which are hidden around the corner of the hallway, and in no time at all we are through the side door and running down the dark, quiet streets of the town.

Lyssa falls into an easy lope beside me. She isn't breathing hard and her smile shines in the brilliant light from the full moon. As we crest the last hill before the forest, her eyes get big and her mouth opens in a round, silent "oh". I turn to follow her gaze and a form emerges from the darkness of the treeline like a part of the night is breaking away from the forest and running flat out in our direction.

Lyssa falters and fights to slow her momentum as the creature barrels toward us. She wraps her hand around my wrist and scrambles backwards, dragging us away from the rampaging beast.

Two hundred pounds of fur and muscle hit me, sending my body rolling across the grass. I come to an abrupt stop, flat on my back looking up at a huge gaping muzzle. A long pink tongue rolls out and drool splatters onto my forehead.

"Off!" I laugh, pushing ineffectually at Shadow's wide chest. My fingers sink into his coarse, thick hair in what is more a pet than an actual push. The cooperative beast rolls onto his side anyway and is soon writhing in the grass, four huge feet in the air as I rub his belly.

Remembering Lyssa, I look up to find her staring at us in shock. Meeting my smiling eyes she snaps her mouth shut and squints, crossing her arms.

"I thought you were being attacked," she bites out.

"I was," I point out helpfully, still rubbing my assailant's exposed belly.

"I'm going to go out on a limb here," Lyssa says primly, "and assume you are acquainted with this creature."

"I am," I smile.

Lyssa steps closer, her curiosity winning out over her pique.

"Does he have a name?" she asks, moving to kneel at my side.

"His name is Shadow, and he is my very best friend."

Lyssa pulls back and looks at me with wide eyes. "I thought I was your best friend," she says, pushing to her feet.

"I'm sorry, I shouldn't have said that." She looks down, brushing at her dress and backing away. I leap up, following her.

"You are!" I reach out a hand. "He's a different kind of friend. He runs with me in the forest and we hunt together. Sometimes he sleeps curled up beside me. But he's not like me."

"I'm not like you either," Lyssa points out. Her arms are crossed over her chest and her face has fallen into sad lines.

"You feel like me," I tell her simply.

"I do?"

"You feel like the other part of me." I hold out my hand and wait. I'm not anxious or worried. Because I know what I said is true.

Lyssa's face softens, the sad lines melting away as her eyes glisten with unshed tears. She moves back toward me slowly, reaching out to take my hand. I tug her closer when she hesitates at arm's length and her arms slip around my waist.

Lyssa's body shudders in my arms as she begins to cry and I lean my head against hers, the soft silk of her hair against my cheek. I listen to our hearts beating and wait for the storm to pass.

Chapter Seventeen

Shadow slaps the grass near Lyssa's crossed legs, causing her to jump and give a high-pitched giggle. His tongue flops out of his mouth and he rolls onto his back to paw at her awkwardly while upside down.

"What does he want?" She's smiling at the ridiculous beast but still trying to angle her body away from his antics.

"Hands," I shrug.

"He wants to have hands?"

"Your hands!" I laugh at her.

She giggles. "He wants to eat my hands?" I love that she's being silly.

"No, you goose! He wants you to touch him with your hands," I roll my eyes at her from where I'm lying on the grass. I know my smile is as goofy as Shadow's as the two of them learn to play together.

Lyssa hovers a hand over the domed furry chest, her eyes tracking his every movement. "Where?"

"Anywhere! He likes hands." I scoot closer to them and place my hand over hers, moving it onto the arch of Shadow's chest. "Here."

Our fingers move through his course-soft fur and he groans in delight, causing us both to giggle again.

"I've never seen a wolf in person before," Lyssa admits, "but I'm almost positive they aren't supposed to be this big."

I shrug. "He is the biggest."

"There are others?" Lyssa looks around as if they might pop out of the trees at any moment.

"His mother lives in the forest," I explain . "She has had many babies, but none are like Shadow."

"Interesting," she mumbles, tapping her chin with the hand not buried in Shadow's fur. "I wonder if he had a different father. He almost looks like a direwolf, but those are supposed to be extinct."

Shadow waves his huge paws in the air at Lyssa and she obediently runs her hand through the hair on his chest. I show her the spots on his chin that he likes scratched. Eventually he rolls over and we both rub his big, tufted ears and the back of his neck.

The two of us are huddled together over Shadow's big block head, which takes up the entirety of my lap, when a soft howl echoes through the night. Shadow immediately bounds to his feet and lifts his head to answer the call. He turns back, offering us each a quick swipe of the tongue before disappearing into the trees.

"Ugh!" Lyssa cries, wiping at her cheek.

I snicker at her shudders of disgust and she plucks a buttercup from the grass at her hip and throws it at me. The soft little flower flutters into my lap and I laugh even harder.

Lyssa launches herself at me with a cute little growl, taking us both to the ground. After a moment she tires of trying to kill me while I giggle inanely, and she flops onto the grass beside me, our shoulders pressed together.

I close my eyes and sigh. The night is warm and the grass is cool and I am happy.

"Do you think that was Shadow's mother calling?" Lyssa asks softly.

"Yes." I open my eyes to gaze up at the stars. She doesn't say anything else so I turn my head to study her profile. Lyssa is searching the night sky, her brow furrowed. I roll onto my side, tucking my hands under my cheek.

"Do you remember your mother?" she asks.

"Yes." I pause. "A little."

Lyssa turns toward me, mirroring my position.

"What do you remember?"

Our noses are less than a handspan apart and I close my eyes to think about her question.

"I remember her wearing pretty dresses," I begin slowly. "I remember her calling me her darling girl and I remember sitting on the floor while she talked to people or did needlework. I remember her holding my hand as we walked in the town."

I hesitate, my voice caught in my throat. I remember how pale her face was when I bit her. How she tried to talk in her firm voice but her hands were shaking. But I don't say that.

"I don't remember my mother ever holding my hand," Lyssa says, distracting me from my own memories. "I had several different nannies. They didn't seem to stay long. There used to be more staff at the house but they all left too. When the last nanny left, my mother decided I was old enough that I didn't need one anymore and she just left Marie." Lyssa closes her eyes. "Marie promised me she'd stay with me until the end."

"You're not sick anymore." I reach out to touch her arm.

Lyssa's eyes pop open and she meets my gaze, frowning. "So now I'll have a long miserable life as Lady Mannix."

"No, you will not."

Lyssa pulls away from me to sit up, legs crossed. She sighs and squares her shoulders.

"What are you suggesting? That I run away to live in the forest with you?" Her expression is tight and her eyes hard.

"I don't live in the forest," I point out. "I have a house."

"You do?" She seems startled. Had she thought I slept beneath the trees or in a cave?

"Yes." I cock my head at her. "Would you like to see it?"

Lyssa waffles for a moment.

"I would," she says finally, "but it's getting late—or early, as the case may be—and I need to get back to my room before the household wakes." Her expression softens. "Will you show me tomorrow?"

It is an hour before dawn when we sneak Lyssa back into her room and the big house is finally dark. Nothing stirs inside. I help her unbutton the brown dress and then slip away to run through the night.

The air is soft and cool as it caresses my warm cheeks, and I let myself sink back into the memories of my mother.

When I first woke up in the blackened husk of my house, I thought my mother left me because I'd been bad. Now I knew that there must have been a fire and that my mother was almost certainly dead. She would not have left me. Even if she was afraid of me.

I have seen Lyssa's parents and I have seen how they looked at their daughter. There is no warmth or affection in their eyes. They do not love their daughter.

I knew that even if my mother was afraid, she did not leave me.

My mother loved me.

I wander through our house, trying to remember how each room looked before that night when I woke up alone, trying to piece together my memories. In most of my dreams the house is full of light and color, but sometimes it is dark and quiet and my mother sits beside my bed, her face pale and streaked with tears.

Had I been sick like Lyssa? I remember lying in the bed, my mother crying. I remember my skin burning. It was like the morning I tried to stay up for the sun.

That is one of my last memories before I woke up alone.

Walking back into my room I curl up on the floor, the dawn dragging me into a deep, dreamless sleep.

Chapter Eighteen

I wake up the next evening with Shadow curled against my back, snoring softly. He shakes himself awake when I rise and the two of us set off into the night. We each catch our dinner, but when Shadow hunkers down to enjoy his meal, I leave him behind and drain mine on the run, leaving the empty husk at the edge of the forest.

There is another party at Lyssa's house and the garden is full of ladies in colorful dresses. The gas lights are lit but everyone is distracted. The guests chat and dance and the staff runs to and fro carrying heavy platters of treats and trays of drinks. It is easy to slip through the side door and up the back staircase to Lyssa's room.

I pause and listen at the door for a moment before slipping inside. The room is dark and the bed empty. I freeze, swept by panic, and my heart stutters. Then a small movement draws my eyes to the window and I can breathe again.

Lyssa stands framed against the night, her long hair reflecting the silver of the stars against the black sky.

"Lyssa?" I whisper. "Why are you in the dark?"

I know she can hear me. After a moment I move to stand by her side. The light from below casts a faint golden glow against Lyssa's face as she stares down at the partygoers infesting the garden. Her skin looks like silk along the curve of her cheek, but the muscle beneath her jaw is throbbing with tension. Her fingers are clenched around the window sill.

Patience has never been my strong suit, but I know better than to poke at a beehive. Lyssa is vibrating. I am almost positive her anger isn't directed at me, and I want to keep it that way, so I stand quietly and let her seethe.

Without turning to me, Lyssa grinds out, "Do you see this?" She nods at the brightly dressed women and black-suited men moving about the garden, between tables laden with food and evenly spaced braziers. "Do you see this party?"

She isn't looking at me, but I nod.

"This is my engagement party," she bites out.

I freeze, unable to formulate a response and afraid to reach out to her in this mood.

Lyssa pushes away from the window and turns back to the dark room. She sits on the bed and drops her head into her hands, trembling. I follow more slowly and sit down beside her.

There is a tray of small iced biscuits on the table and I pull it onto my lap. I sit beside Lyssa as she gathers herself, and methodically bite my finger over and over again to decorate each of the biscuits with my blood, except for the last one, which I pop into my mouth.

Still chewing, I offer the first biscuit to Lyssa, holding it in her line of sight. She looks up as she accepts the offering and I make a production of chewing the cooking in my mouth, eliciting a half-hearted giggle. I swallow my treat and smile as Lyssa eats, holding a hand over her lips as she giggles while chewing.

"Don't choke," I admonish her, still smiling.

"I wouldn't do them the favor of choking to death on a biscuit," she announces, her nose in the air.

We both break into giggles, our shoulders touching. My chest is lighter, but I am still worried. As Lyssa's giggles wind down her face falls and tears glistening in her eyes.

"I hate them," she confesses, popping another blood-laced cookie into her mouth. She reaches over and turns up the lamp on her table, casting the room in a soft glow. "I didn't want them to see me."

"We can go," I tell her. "We can run away right now, this very minute."

Lyssa sits there as thoughts grind away behind her eyes. Her lips purse and her face takes on a serious cast.

"We need a plan," she announces, hopping to her feet.

"Come to my house," I urge her.

"It isn't far enough away, Sharptooth." Lyssa shakes her head. "They'll find us there and bring me back."

All I really know is the forest and I've never ventured far from it. This town is the furthest I have ever traveled. I am vaguely aware that there are similar towns to the north, and great, snow-capped mountains to the south. Beyond the town is a sea, upon which I'd once seen a magnificent ship with huge, white sails.

"What would be far enough?" I ask Lyssa now. "The ships cross the sea..." I trail off, shrugging. In my mind I imagine them sailing off the edge of the world. I can't picture what could be on the other side of the vast waters. More forests? More towns? Mountains?

"The sea?" Lyssa asked. She cocks her head, considering. "There are colonies across the ocean. My father's ships send goods back and forth. I've read about them and they seem quite wild. There are tales of strange peoples and great beasts."

"Could Shadow come?" I ask.

Lyssa barks out a laugh. "Two strange girls and a great beast...Why not?"

Chapter Nineteen

I follow Lyssa from the dimly lit room, out into the bright hallway. Gas lights project from the wall, flickering madly, as we make our way to the first level of the house. Lyssa walks with confidence, despite the sounds of the party still going on in the garden. I follow more cautiously, slipping around corners and moving from shadow to shadow.

Lyssa stops at a pair of tall wood doors, flinging them open. I duck behind the door as gasps echo from within the room.

"Get out," Lyssa says abruptly, her voice harsher than I've ever heard it.

"Well, I never," declares a feminine voice from within. "Who exactly are you?"

"The bride," Lyssa growls.

There is a beat of silence and then scurrying as two young women in beaded gowns beat feet out of the room and back toward the garden. Their heads are bent toward each other and I can hear their excited whispers. Once they are out of sight, I slide from my hiding spot and enter the room, pulling the large doors shut behind me.

Lyssa is standing before a wall of bookshelves, pulling small leather bound tomes from the shelves. She glances over her shoulder at me, waving me forward.

"There's one more I need to find. I know it's here somewhere." Lyssa plops her stack of books into my arms and turns back to the shelf as footsteps echo in the hallway.

"Someone's coming," I tell her, darting behind the large leather chair in the corner.

"Let them," she mutters under her breath, still pursuing the shelves of books.

I grasp at her skirts to pull her down into my hiding spot but Lyssa flounces away. I retreat as the doors open.

"Hello, my dear," says a deep, rolling voice. It's Mannix . I tense, ready to leap from my hiding spot.

Lyssa moves back toward me, the skirt of her gown providing additional coverage as I crouch behind the chair. She's given Mannix her back and seems focused on the bookshelf.

"Look at me," he says in that smooth voice that makes my blood run cold.

Lyssa ignores him, running her hand over the spines of the books on the shelf in front of her.

"Look at me!" The smooth glass of his voice has splintered into a thousand cracks, each one raking its razor sharp edge along my skin.

Lyssa freezes. Her body shudders and she grips the shelf in front of her. For a moment it looks as if she is going to turn and then her spine straightens.

"No," she replies. Her knuckles are white where she clutches at the edge of the shelf but her voice doesn't waver.

"Well, well, well," Mannix croons. The smooth voice is back. "This will be interesting." Each word lands like a drip of acid.

He takes a step as his name rings out down the hall announcing the arrival of his coach. There is silence for a moment, then he says, "Soon, my dear," and is gone.

Lyssa's entire body sags and she sinks to the carpet in a puddle of skirts. I pull her into my arms, rocking her as she winds her arms around my waist. My heart is thundering in my chest.

"His voice burned across my skin," she gasps into my shoulder.

"I could feel it too."

Lyssa's breathing steadies and she pulls back enough to meet my eyes, her hands still clutching the fabric of my dress at my waist.

"What is he?" she asks.

"A monster ," I answer. "Like me."

Chapter Twenty

I keep to the shadows as I follow Mannix's flashy black and red carriage through the cobblestone streets. Once we leave the town behind, I drop back further to stay out of sight—and almost miss the carriage turning onto a private lane set between two large elms.

After several minutes the carriage approaches a stone arch with a wrought iron gate. The grounds are teeming with uniformed staff carrying lanterns and two men run forward to open the gate. The facade of a large country house is visible through the archway. It is easily three times the size of mine, with two wings and a sweeping staircase to the front door.

The carriage stops before the house and Mannix disembarks on his own, ignoring the footman in matching black and red livery who offers him a hand. Another uniformed man descends the stairs and approaches the lord, a silver tray held before him.

"A refreshment, My Lord," he offers, and Mannix plucks a small glass from the tray and tips its contents down his throat in one swallow.

"Excellent, Fields. Just what I needed." Mannix drops the glass back on the tray carelessly and his man deftly saves it from rolling to the ground as they both disappear into the house.

I set off into the woods to follow the stone wall around the house. The exterior of the wall has been rendered smooth, leaving no depressions to make it easy to scale. At the rear of the house there is another gate, and a smattering of outbuildings. There is much less activity at this end of the property and I make short work of swinging myself over the iron spikes.

A boy rounds the back of the house leading the carriage horses and I duck behind one of the wood buildings. He disappears into the stables as the breeze shifts in my direction.

I recognize that smell.

Rising carefully, I peer through the window of the building I am leaning against and look into a nightmare.

The interior of the building is bare wooden boards and exposed beams. The dirt floor is darkest toward the middle, churned up and stained almost black. Bales of hay are stacked along one wall and a rusty metal chain hangs from the ceiling, glinting dully in the dim light.

At first I think a dress is hanging from the chain, long strips of filthy fabric falling limply down to puddle onto the floor. But among the folds of material is a dusky bare foot.

I stare at that foot, willing it to move or wiggle or something to show signs of life. Her arms—for there is a woman in the dress—are tied above her head and her hair is hanging over her face. Her weight is on her arms and the tip of her toes barely graze the floor.

The foot doesn't move.

Crouching back down beneath the window, I rush to the front of the building while there is no one in sight. This appears to be some kind of storage shed with a simple pin and bar door catch. I lift the bar from its cradle and the door swings open easily.

I slip into the shed and pull the door closed behind me, hearing the bar drop into place. Glancing back I realize there is no handle on this side, so I'll have to break the door to leave, or climb out of the window. Either way, I'm not concerned.

The meager moonlight that reaches the interior of the shed is enough for my eyes to make out the form of the woman and once again I stare, willing her to move. She is dead or she is alive. Either way I will have to decide what to do. Either way, it is bad. There is no doubt in my mind that Mannix did this to her.

The unknowing is worse than any of the decisions before me, so I gather my nerve and step closer. Reaching out my hand, I carefully sweep the woman's hair to the side. I crouch down to get a better look at her shadowed face, and end up sitting in the dirt when her eyes pop open.

I wait for the woman to react, to scream or cry or beg for help. She stares straight ahead. I shift to the right and her eyes do not follow me.

As I shift, I put my hand down in the dirt–which I now realize is mud. Wiping my hand on the skirt of my dress, I notice the dark stain left behind and lift my fingers to my nose. Blood. My eyes flick back up to the woman hanging above me.

The sound of voices outside launches me to my feet. I scramble behind the hay bale in the corner, wedging myself between the hay and the wood panels of the shed wall as the door creaks open. Above me, the dancing flames of a lantern reflect against the roof of the shed and multiple footsteps sound softly in the dirt. There are at least three people. The window is on the wall opposite me and the new arrivals are between me and the door. I tense my hands, long black claws ready to fight my way out of the room.

"Excellent!" booms Mannix's deep voice into the silence. "She's still alive. This one has lasted much longer than I expected." More footsteps pad across the dirt. "Mmmm," he ponders. "I do think we're coming to the end, though. Such a shame."

"Shall we perform the ritual again, My Lord," asks a dry voice, raspy and thin.

"Yes, Charles. One more time, I think, and our guest will be depleted ."

There is the sound of shuffling and then several voices together begin to sing in an unfamiliar language. It is a low, flat kind of song and it buzzes along my skin like electricity in the air after a lightning strike. I keep my eyes on the ceiling of the shed, where the lantern light dances without rhythm. The light moves one way and the other, dimming, then getting brighter with no discernible pattern. The song becomes louder and my eyes track the light as it gets brighter and brighter. My skin is hot and the ceiling spins.

I wake up with my face pressed into a hay bale, straw poking my cheek and scratching against my neck. My skin is warm and tight and as I push myself up I notice that my blackened claws seem longer than usual.

Despite the position I find myself in, I am fine. Better than fine, even. I am good. I am as strong and warm as if I've drained ten large hares.

There are no signs of movement in the shed and the ceiling is dark. I peek around the hay bale, but there is no sign of the lantern or the men I'd heard before. Mannix is gone.

The woman still hangs in the middle of the shed's open space in exactly the same position.

Crawling out from my hiding spot, I crouch down before her, looking up into her dark face. Her eyes are closed and she is still. I reach up and touch her cheek.

She is cold.

I shiver, and an answering cold moves across my own skin. The woman is a husk now. She has no marks, no holes, no signs that teeth or claws have touched her—but she is drained all the same.

Chapter Twenty-One

I race the sun back to my house, the air rushing past me stealing the tears from my face. I'm not crying for the woman in Mannix's shed. I didn't know her and I am no stranger to death.

These are tears of fear. Lyssa's parents want to tie her to that monster, to send her to live in that house. I run flat out, taking in sobbing breaths, and slam through my door as the first rays of sunlight peek over the hills. I crawl into my room and curl into my spot, holding myself tightly, arms wrapped around my middle, and rock myself to sleep.

I don't dream, but I wake with a sense of the day's passing and a distance from the previous night's terror that brings me perspective. I have only two goals. First and foremost, Lyssa must be stronger. No matter what we face, she will need every advantage. Secondly, I have to convince her to run.

Lyssa's house is once again ablaze with light, glowing against the night sky. There is no one in the garden as I pass by, slipping in the side door and stealing up the servant's stairs. I listen at Lyssa's door for a moment, then quietly let myself into her room.

She's sitting up in the bed, books spilled across the blanket. She has one small book open in her lap and another raised in her hand as she reads from the page. The light on her bedside table gilds her skin and hair, casting a warm glow that isn't there in the moonlight. She turns to look toward me, her eyes unsurprised and warm with welcome.

I climb onto the bed and try to gather my thoughts.

"I followed Mannix to his house." My voice wavers and Lyssa's smile falls. She reaches for my hand and I take hers gratefully. "There was a woman there..."

"A woman?" she asks, arching a brow.

"Not like that," I dismiss. "She was chained up in a shed behind the house." I didn't mean to say it quite so baldly, but perhaps it is for the best. Mannix isn't some charming philanderer. He is a murderer.

"Mannix killed her. She's dead."

Lyssa is struck dumb, her thoughts turning over behind her eyes. "You saw this?"

"I was hiding, but I was in the room. I heard him."

"You heard him what?" Lyssa presses.

I sigh and release her hand, sitting back on the bed to gather my thoughts.

"There was blood on the ground beneath her but I didn't see any wounds." I run my fingers over the spines of the books on the bed between us. "I hid when he came in. He wasn't alone. They sang a song with strange words and the woman died."

Lyssa sits quietly for a moment, absorbing my words. "Strange words? Like a ritual?"

"Yes," I gasp, remembering. "That's the word they used." I frown. "It felt warm, like blood. They sang and her life filled the room with warmth and strength. It was too much. Everything went black."

"It felt like when you drink from an animal?"

"Yes, like that, but more." I hold out my hands. "Look."

We both look down at my black-tipped claws, which are noticeably longer than before. Lyssa grasps one of my hands firmly. Her skin is pink next to mine and her nails are a dusky rose, like the petals in the garden below her window. My nails are black and take over the whole of my fingertip, extending out to a tip.

"Fascinating," she murmurs, running one pink finger along the tip of one of my sharp black claws.

"Mannix is dangerous," I point out. "We must run."

Lyssa releases my hand and gestures to the books around her.

"I've been working on that," she says. "These books are the records that my father's company compiled about the western colonies, and this is a journal from a young man who went on mission there not too long ago. I've been comparing the two." Lyssa glances down at the small book in her lap, frowning. "There are quite a few discrepancies, actually."

"You need to be stronger." I don't know anything about the colonies, but this I'm sure about.

Lyssa sighs. "Yes, I know." She looks about vaguely. "I could ring down to the kitchen for sweets. Marie is likely serving my parents dinner at the moment but I'm sure one of the new girls would bring them up."

"We don't really need the sweets," I point out carefully.

Lyssa doesn't respond, so I bite the end of my finger and squeeze a bead of blood out of the tip. I hold the tiny droplet of blood out to her and she touches it gently, transferring it to her own pink finger. I'm mesmerized as she raises her finger to her lips.

We both jump at the soft knock at the door. Marie's voice calls Lyssa's name as the hinges begin to creek. I throw myself over the far side of the bed, rolling beneath the high mattress, my heart pounding.

"I've brought you some of the extra scones from dinner, Miss," Marie tells Lyssa. "Your parents hardly touched them and I thought you might enjoy them. You've been doing so much better lately."

"Thank you, Marie!" Lyssa gushes, sounding slightly out of breath. "They're perfect. I was just thinking that I could eat something."

There is shuffling and then Marie exclaims, "Oh, dear, Miss! Did you hurt yourself?"

"Oh no, I'm fine, Marie," Lyssa replies. "That's from my friend, Sharptooth," she laughs.

After a long silence the door squeaks and I roll out from under the bed. Lyssa's head appears above me, hanging off the side of the mattress. Our eyes meet and we dissolve into giggles.

By the time I get myself off of the floor and back onto the bed, Lyssa has stacked her books off to the side and placed the plate of buttery pastries between us.

I christen each one in my bright red blood and Lyssa eats them under my watchful eye.

Chapter Twenty-Two

Once again the garden is full of colorful dresses and black suits. I am hiding behind a rose bush, making my way toward where Lyssa is seated at a large round table.

Her back straight and her hands folded in her lap, she looks like she is ready to bolt at any moment. The other occupants of the table speak over her, ignoring her discomfort. As I move closer I can hear her parents arguing with each other. The fourth figure at the table, Lord Mannix, is sitting back and observing them all with a speculative gleam in his eye.

"The sooner the better, I say," blusters Lyssa's father. The guests around them glance at his tone but look away quickly.

Lyssa's mother waves her hand at him, "Lower your voice, Charles. It is unseemly...as is too much haste in such things." The woman touches an elegant hand to the icy blonde hair piled high upon her head as she shoots covert looks at the guests around them. "We are already the talk of the town due to her age," she continues. "There is no point in rushing the ceremony."

Her husband leans toward her over the table and lowers his voice from a roar to a shout. "There is a lot riding on this merger. We can't risk the chance that the girl's *health*," he nods in Lyssa's direction with eyebrows raised, "scuppers the whole deal."

"She's actually doing much better, Charles, surely even you can see that." She waves toward Lyssa as if she is a painting under discussion.

And Lyssa sits like a painting, showing no sign that she is following the conversation at all.

I move around a lush fern of some sort until I am directly behind Lyssa's chair, hidden in the shadows of the large leaves. I reach out carefully and place my hand over hers in her lap. She jumps and looks up to scan the faces around her to make sure no one is looking her way. Then she turns her hand in mine and grips it firmly.

"Mother," Lyssa interrupts her father as he continues to argue. "I think it's time I retire for the evening. May I be excused?"

Her mother doesn't even look at her, just waves her hand generally in her direction. Lyssa lets my fingers slide from her grasp as she stands and I slip back into the shadows.

I make my way along the outside of the garden and follow Lyssa into the house. As the door falls closed behind me, something draws my eyes back to the table.

Mannix is looking right at me.

The door cuts off his gaze and I hurry up the stairs behind Lyssa.

I'm huddled under the bed, my mouth full of shortbread as Marie bustles around the bedroom, fussing over Lyssa.

"You need to be more careful, Miss," the older woman tells her.

"I swear, Marie, it wasn't my blood. I'm totally fine," Lyssa assures her again.

"Oh, no more of this invisible friend nonsense!"

"It isn't nonsense, Marie." There is silence for a long moment and then Lyssa speaks more softly. "Do you promise not to tell my parents?"

"You know you can tell me anything, Miss Lyssa. It's been just you and me here for so long."

"I know you work for my parents," Lyssa hedges.

The bed creaks as Marie lowers her weight onto it.

"I made you a promise years ago, Miss. You won't be alone when the end comes."

"I'm getting better, Marie. Surely you must see that," Lyssa protests.

"Well, certainly, you have had some good days these last few weeks—and I am so happy about that—but you must accept that this is temporary and try to enjoy the time that you have," Marie cautions, her voice gentle. "My own mother died of the wasting disease. She had her good days too, but it always wins in the end, my dear."

"Sharptooth is curing me," Lyssa insists, her voice rising with frustration. Her bare feet appear in my line of sight, visible in the small gap between the floor and the bedskirt.

"Look at me, Marie!" The feet twirl. "I'm better! I can stand and walk and run through the forest!"

"The forest?" Marie gasps. "You've been out of the house? Alone?"

"No! That's what I'm telling you. I wasn't alone."

The bedskirt lifts and an eye appears.

"She doesn't believe me. Come out."

I'm not sure this is a good idea, but there's no point in hiding now. I slither out from under the bed, using my arms to push myself up like a cobra. Marie must think so too, because the woman looks at me as if I'm about to bite her.

I make the situation much worse by smiling.

Marie hits the floor with a thud and Lyssa gasps.

"Oh, for goodness sake," Lyssa cries, exasperated with both of us.

I am summarily shooed from the room, the door closing firmly behind me as Lyssa turns to take care of her incapacitated maid. I huff as I slip down the stairs and out into the night.

Shadow is waiting for me outside of the house and is quite disappointed when I appear empty-handed, but he stays by my side as we run all the way home. It isn't late but I'm tired, as I am on the nights I bleed for Lyssa. By the time the dark outline of my house looms in the distance, I am ready to curl up in my dark room.

The figure of Lord Mannix standing before the steps to my house is not a welcome sight.

I hesitate at the top of the hill and gesture to Shadow to stay back. He cuts to the left and runs off along the treeline. I continue forward at a much slower pace.

It is tempting to try to run away, but he is standing in front of *my* house. Where would I go? I could go back to Lyssa's, but he must have seen me there. There is no point in trying to hide. And there is no reason to. I am not afraid.

Mannix may be a monster, but so am I.

Chapter Twenty-Three

When I run I lean forward, keeping low to the ground, but now I stand up straight. I walk up to my house as my mother would have, my head held high.

"You look just like her," Mannix says.

"Like who?" I ask, although I know the answer. I pause at the edge of the courtyard. Too far away for normal conversation, but Mannix seems to have no trouble hearing me.

"Amelia," he says. "Your mother."

Amelia . Amelia. Did I know her name was Amelia? I don't think so, but now the name echoes through my head on a loop, as if I've always known it. As if it has been waiting in the dark for the right time to come forward. *Amelia.*

"She tried to leave me," Mannix continues, but I'm not listening.

"You knew my mother? Do you know what happened to her?"

"She's dead," he says baldly.

It isn't really unexpected, but I still flinch.

"In the fire?" I ask, my eyes drifting away from his tall figure to roam over the charred walls of the house behind him.

"Yes," he confirms. "The fool ran into the burning house." Mannix looks at me consideringly. "Although I suppose that makes more sense now."

"How did you know her?"

"She was my wife," he announces, sweeping his hand to the side in a throwaway gesture.

The world seems to hold its breath.

"Are you my father?"

Mannix bursts into laughter and my face heats. Had I been presumptuous? Is it ridiculous for a girl who runs through the forest on bare feet to fancy herself the lost child of a lord?

I am on the verge of turning to flee back into the forest when Mannix bursts out, "Of course I am."

I stare at him, the gears in my head ground to a halt.

"Did you think you inherited those teeth from your mother?" Mannix sneers at me.

"I bit my mother," I say numbly, my brain still stuttering over his revelations.

"Of course you did. You're an abomination," Mannix dismisses.

A flare of rage sparks to life inside me.

"So are you," I fling at him. "I've been to your house. I saw the woman you killed."

"Did you?" he asks mildly. "And what did you think?"

"I thought you were a monster!"

"Did you?" he asks again, this time with a sneer. "Have you never killed, child? I don't believe that for a moment." Mannix begins walking toward me, across the courtyard. "The fact that you stand here alive before me proves that you are no innocent ."

"I hunt in the forest, like everything else that lives there." I tell him, lifting my chin and watching him closely as he approaches. "I don't kill for fun. I don't kill people." I fix him with my fiercest stare. "You are a murderer."

"So dramatic," Mannix mocks. "Trust me, child, you would have been as well, had you lived."

With that Mannix launches himself at me. I roll to the side, dimly aware of the pain in my teeth and claws as they lengthen. He is nearly twice my size, but I am fueled by my rage.

Mannix catches my shoulder, sending us into a roll as his claws rip through my pretty dress and the skin under it. Sky and trees flash by as we tumble across the grass, but I focus on the man trying to kill me. Ignoring the pain at my shoulder, I sink my claws into his chest and go for his throat with my teeth.

Some of the beasts in the forest are familiar with the men who hunt there with arrows and rifles. They will sometimes mistake me for one of them–a smaller and weaker version. I imagine they have enough time to feel surprise before they die, and to wonder what I am. Lord Mannix knows what I am, but his eyes still widen in shock as I pull away from his throat, my mouth full of his blood.

He flings me away and I am airborne for a long moment that ends abruptly with a crack that reverberates through the night. I have hit a tree and am paralyzed by the pain that floods my body.

Mannix stalks to me, one hand raised above his head, claws already glistening with my blood. An image of Lyssa flashes into my head. Her arms are bound over her head and she is hanging from the chain in Mannix's shed, her long silvery hair falling over her downbent head.

I push myself away from the tree, only to flop over onto the grass as parts of my body refuse to respond to my pleas. I roll again, onto my back, and raise one clawed hand as Mannix leans over me.

A dark blur comes crashing from the side, gleaming white teeth clamping around the lord's arm, spinning him away from me. I let myself collapse back onto the ground, giving into the pain for a moment. Gritting my teeth, I turn my head to track the bodies rolling through the grass.

Shadow stands over Mannix, who is screaming hoarsely. The wolf tosses his huge black head and Mannix screams again, his voice breaking as it pierces through the night. It takes me a moment to process what I am seeing. Shadow has a long shape in his jaws.

It is Mannix's arm.

Mannix is still making that horrible sound, his legs flailing as he scrambles out from under the wolf. His remaining arm is behind him, clawing at the dirt. He flips over and a second later he is on his feet and disappearing into the forest.

Shadow looks torn. He glances back at me, then at the spot in the darkness where Mannix vanished. Finally he spits out his grotesque trophy and huffs a sigh before trotting over to my side.

I haven't moved from where I'd fallen. Everything hurts.

Shadow looks down at me with a furrowed brow, whining softly. I reach up a hand to touch his face and pain pierces my brain.

The next thing I know, I'm opening my eyes to the night sky. I shift my head gingerly to find that I haven't moved from my place in the grass at the edge of the courtyard.

Shadow appears from the trees, a fat hare in his jaws. He slows as he approaches me, meeting my gaze. He places the hare carefully beside my head and sits back on his haunches to stare at me intently.

Very, very slowly, I turn my head until my nose is buried in the still warm fur of the hare's hide. Even my teeth hurt as I sink them through the thick skin, but the moment my mouth floods with blood the pain begins to recede.

By the time I have drained that hare, Shadow is dropping another beside me. This time I am strong enough to bring up my hand to hold it in place as I devour the second hare...and the third. Soon I am able to sit up, my body tingling and my head still spinning in exhaustion. I lean against Shadow's side, wiping blood and the crust of dried tears from my face.

I desperately need to get back to Lyssa but I can't even sit upright on my own. My fingers curl into Shadow's fur as frustration and fear clench around my heart.

Shadow whines and I lift my head to look at him. He's saved me twice already, but the sun is approaching and I need his help again. I have to survive this night in order to help Lyssa. My only consolation is that Mannix is too injured to do anything tonight. If he is the same as me, he'll be forced to go to ground at dawn as well. I have to believe that Lyssa will be safe until I can get back to her.

Gathering my energy, I sink my hand into the fur at the back of Shadow's neck and pull myself up with all of my strength. He holds still as I rise, inch by inch, to my feet. As my knees begin to wobble, Shadow ducks down and moves into me, causing me to collapse across his back.

Immediately he bounds up and takes off into the trees, with me clinging to his back. Under other circumstances, this would have been amazing. Instead I focus all of my strength on my fingers clutching desperately at his fur. Every step is a sledgehammer to my body and my head tosses to and fro. I cling to Shadow and consciousness with equal tenacity.

When my trusty steed's steps finally slow I realize that I've had my eyes screwed closed for most of the wild ride. Shadow comes to a stop and lowers to the ground, my dangling feet hitting a hard surface. With effort I force open my eyes to complete darkness.

After a frozen moment, there are shapes in the darkness and the edges of rock glistening faintly with moisture in the meager light around the small entrance. We are in a cave.

I relax my fingers, one by one, from their deathgrip on Shadow's fur and let myself slide down to the stone floor. It is bliss. The light coming through the opening shifts slowly from silver to yellow. As it brightens, Shadow moves his bluk in front of the opening, casting the small cave into total darkness.

There are so many things I needed to remember. What Mannix said, what he was. *Lyssa.* Thoughts swirl around my mind, just out of reach.

My eyes fall closed and I drift away.

Chapter Twenty-Four

I wake to complete darkness. *Lyssa.* Reaching out a hand to sweep it before me, I encounter Shadow's warm body. He moves with my touch, shifting away from the cave's entrance and allowing the pale moonlight to edge everything in silver. *Lyssa.* I slither past him, out of the cave.

Lyssa. Lyssa. Lyssa. My brain beats with her name from the moment I open my eyes.

Shadow follows behind me as I crash through the forest without my usual grace. The small warm things are smart enough to flee my path of destruction, but I startle a healthy young doe and drink my fill before continuing on.

My limbs have regained their strength. Nothing hurts.

Lyssa.

How long was I asleep? How many hours have passed?

We move through the fields and into the town, flying over cobblestone streets. I don't hesitate at the door to the house. The time for subtlety has passed. Marie saw me. Mannix knows what I am. When the knob doesn't turn, a well-placed kick beside it flings the door back on its hinges and I am flying up the stairs, calling her name.

"Lyssa?" There is no response, no sense of movement from anywhere in the house. Lyssa's door crashes back against the wall and I stand frozen in the entryway.

The room is completely empty.

Not only empty of Lyssa, but empty of everything. There is no bed, no armoire , no table, no chair, no paintings on the wall or curtains on the windows. Everything is gone.

I'm not aware of Shadow behind me until he noses me out of the way to enter the room. He sniffs along the barren floor, tracing the faint outline left by the rug that used to sit under Lyssa's big bed, where we had sat and ate sweets and giggled at each other.

The blood that was pounding her name through my head rushes away as if the drain is being pulled in a tub. I collapse onto the floor at the doorway of the empty room, my brain completely empty. I have no plans, no ideas.

Lyssa is gone.

I don't have the first clue where to even start looking for her. I know her parents came from the city and I have a general idea where that is, but it's much further than I've ever gone. How will I find her?

Catapulting myself up from the floor, I run down the hall, flinging open doors. Room after room stands empty. Faint outlines mark the missing rugs and furniture, but the house is nothing but a hollowed out husk. Even the library is completely empty, shelf after shelf naked but for the dusty outline left by Lyssa's books. There are no pots or plates in the kitchen, no table or chairs in the dining room. No clues, no hints of where she might have gone. There is nothing.

She didn't leave me. I know she wouldn't have left voluntarily. They took her. I have to find her.

I'm standing in the foyer, arms on my akimbo and chest heaving, when Shadow tears past me and through the door. Hope spikes through my chest as I follow in his wake. He runs out of the house and down the street, turning again and again until we find ourselves on a narrow pass between two short rows of plain brown houses.

Nose to the ground, Shadow leads the way to a plain wood door, flanked by shuttered windows. Light leaks around the edges of the window. Glancing back at me, he paws at the ground before the door. Heart pounding, I grab the handle and push it open with enough force to have it rock back on its hinges.

A figure stands before a small hearth, the shadow of their body outlined by the warm yellow light. For a moment my heart swells in my chest, emotion rushing up through my body. Then the woman turns.

Marie. My heart freezes as emotions play across the maid's face. Shock. Fear. Guilt.

I'm across the room in an instant, my hands knotted in the front of Marie's dress.

"Where is she?" I bite out, Shadow growling at my side. The woman screams and begins babbling, nonsense words falling from her lips as she stares up into my face with an expression of pure terror. I shake her, lifting one hand to wrap my long, claw-tipped fingers around her throat. "Where. Is. She." I spit each word into her face as Shadow nips and snarls.

"The city! The city. Her parents took her to the city," Marie babbles. She is crying now, chest heaving.

"Where in the city?" I hiss into her face, unmoved by her terror.

The sharp smell of urine fills the room and I drop the woman in disgust. Shadow sneezes, shaking his head. She sits in a pile on the floor where she fell, her hands clutched before her as she begins to chant some protective prayer.

Spotting a desk sitting in the corner of the room, I grabbed a handful of Marie's hair and dragged her across the room to throw her into the chair sitting before it. I gesture to the paper and quill already sitting out.

"Draw it. Show me how to find her."

A long time later, we exit the small house, a map to Lyssa's location clutched in my hand. I glance up at the moon, judging how much night we have left. It is a long journey and we'll have to hurry to make it before dawn.

The road to the city is clearly marked and nearly empty this time of night. We pass only one carriage, its windows covered. If the driver spots us, he gives no sign. He is likely too busy regaining control of his horses, who balk as we fly by. At one point we spot a camp set back from the road, fires burning, but again we pass them without pausing.

We only stop once, veering off the road to flush two hares from the bush. I drain both and Shadow disposes of the husks, fur and all.

It is perhaps an hour, or slightly less, before dawn, when we approach the outer limits of the city. Here there is much more traffic and lights blazed on every street and in many windows.

I might be able to hide my black-tipped claws and sharp teeth, the tears in my dress...but the extraordinarily large black wolf by my side? That will be harder to explain.

We keep to the dark alleys and side streets as much as possible, moving quickly. I glance at the sky to the east, fearing the arrival of the sun there more than I have anything before in my life, even Mannix. I can't fight the sun. I can only hide from it.

Following Marie's tear-stained map, we work our way north through the city. The salt in the air is sharp as we get closer to the harbor. Finally the streets widen and the houses become taller. Turning at a large, steepled church marked on the map, we crest a hill to come into a neighborhood of houses made of a smooth, flat stone.

Number 54 is at the end of a row and has a small archway leading to the front entry, as Marie described.

The edge of the sky is pale pink and orange to the east as we circle the house. At the rear, a small carriage house sits at the threshold of the alleyway. Spears of yellow are cresting over the tops of the buildings as I muscle my way inside. Shadow follows me closely through the door and I push it shut behind us.

Sunlight spears through a small high window on the south face of the building and tears of frustration run down my face as I crouch under the dilapidated carriage braced against one wall. We are trapped for the day.

Chapter Twenty-Five

Whatever organ it is inside of my body that keeps track of the movement of the sun, it goes off like a church bell the moment full darkness falls upon the city. Shadow is already awake and clawing at the door.

The surrounding homes may be empty or have more frugal owners, for the house belonging to Lyssa's parents is the only one ablaze with light from every window. Tall and thin, the house rises above the wide street with a grand entrance at the top of a large staircase in the front. At the rear of the home is a more modest porch with another door set beneath it.

The lower door gives with a little encouragement and Shadow and I slip inside the house. We're in a small mudroom off of the kitchens, which are empty. I'm trying to be quiet, but I am vibrating with urgency. I will avoid any people in the house that I can, but I will go through them if I can't. I have to find Lyssa.

Now.

Beyond the kitchens a narrow staircase leads to the upper levels. I pause, considering, and head up. On the first landing I freeze as the sound of a doorbell echoes through the house. Fast footsteps followed by muffled voices drift to where we are. The first voice is quiet and smooth. The second voice is a demanding baritone that sends chills through my chest.

Lord Mannix is here.

Whichever member of the staff who has opened the door to Mannix is trying to get him to wait in the salon when Lyssa's mother makes her entrance. Her voice is high and shrill, like nails on a chalkboard. Mannix's low rumble cuts her off as I gesture to Shadow to wait in the stairwell and move silently toward the foyer.

"I came as soon as I received your note, Estelle."

Peeking carefully around the corner, I catch a glimpse of the tableau in the foyer. The black uniformed butler stands silently by as Lyssa's mother gazes up at Mannix, wringing her hands. Beside her, Lyssa's father stands silent, for once. A small man in a black suit with a white collar is quietly watching the exchange. Mannix wears a long black cloak hanging straight down from his shoulders, hiding any sign of injury.

"I find it difficult to believe you abandoned the house based on the word of some silly maid," Mannix continues. "The woman was obviously overwrought with the responsibility of caring for Lyssa's needs."

"Marie has always been completely reliable, My Lord," Lyssa's mother insistes. "And it explains so much! Her sudden improvement...I wanted to believe she was getting better but we all knew it wasn't possible. We'd all accepted that the end was near." Lyssa's mother reaches out to grasp her husband's hand and clutches her other hand to her forehead. "For her to make this sudden recovery, it seemed like a miracle. I was so gullible. I should have known it was the work of the devil!"

"The devil!" gasps Mannix's companion. "Surely you must be mistaken, madam." The man frowns up at Lyssa's mother.

"Lady Estelle, this is Father Francisco," Mannix nods between the two. "He will perform the marriage ceremony and then I shall take Lyssa to my country house where she will be safe from such unsightly influences."

I wonder briefly if he is referring to me or Marie, but either way I know I am running out of time. Lyssa's parents are sputtering protests but they will give in to Mannix's demands. They always do.

I slip back down the hallway and turn into the back stairwell. It's empty. There's no sign of Shadow. I listen intently, looking up and down the stairs, but hear nothing. Pressing my lips together, I continue back up the stairs, heart pounding.

On the next landing the stairs open to a long hallway with doors on either side. No sign of Shadow. Torn, I continue up. Again there is a long hallway, but this time a large black wolf sits calmly before one of the doors. I let out the breath I've been holding, rushing to his side.

"Please don't do that again," I beg, knowing he won't understand. I rub the flat spot on his head between his ears and he leans into my hand for a moment, before turning back to stare at the door he is guarding.

I turn the knob, surprised when it opens without resistance.

Chapter Twenty-Six

"Lyssa!" The silver-haired figure on the bed moves at my call but doesn't turn toward me. "Lyssa, it's me!"

Her shoulders twitch but still she faces stubbornly away, not responding.

I falter, coming to a stop a few feet from the bed.

"Are you mad at me?" I whisper. "I know Marie told your parents and they made you come here."

No response.

"I heard them call me a devil. I don't think that's what I am. Although Mannix says I am his daughter and he certainly is." I stop my rambling. I am definitely not making things better.

Lyssa shifts position, but doesn't acknowledge me. I can tell she's listening and my throat closes up.

"I am a monster," I admit softly. "But I'm your monster." Lyssa's shoulders move again and I wonder if she's crying.

"Please just talk to me, Lyssa," I beg, my own eyes filling with tears. "Tell me to leave and I will. I promise."

Lyssa's shoulders shake and a small sound like a whimper escapes her. Not able to handle the silence any longer, I take the last steps to the bed and reach for her shoulder. The muscles are rigid beneath my hand.

"Lyssa?" I pull on her shoulder, forcing her to face me.

"Lyssa!" Her eyes are open and screaming at me, but her mouth is covered by a white cloth stretched tight between her lips. "What—?" I carefully thread one sharp claw beneath her gag and rip through the material. It falls away, revealing more fabric. I pull and pull as pieces of fabric keep coming from her mouth.

When her mouth is finally empty, Lyssa sobs, "Untie me, untie me! Quick, before they come back."

I rip the bed cover from her body and stand frozen for a moment in shock. She is tied from shoulder to feet, her hands bound behind her back.

"Why?" I ask, as I start tearing at her bonds. "Why did they do this? Who did it? Your parents?"

"Yes," she gasps, carefully bringing one arm forward. I can do nothing to ease her pain as she regains feeling in her limbs. "Marie helped them." Finally she's completely free and Lyssa slowly sits up, grabbing onto my hands.

"Marie was crazy. She went screaming out of my room the second she woke up and told my parents that I'd been consorting with a devil or a demon or some such nonsense."

I pull her to her feet and hold her steady as she wobbles alarmingly.

Lyssa stomps her feet to wake them up. "I fought them," she says, looking into my eyes. "It took Marie and my parents and two other maids for them to tie me up." Lyssa stills. The tears in her eyes have dried. "You are not a monster. You made me better. Stronger . I won't let them take that away."

Her arms are around me and I bury my face in her soft, silver hair.

I could stay like that forever, but Shadow whines urgently from the door and I know we're running out of time.

"We have to get out of here," I say, pulling back but keeping hold of her hand. I tug her toward the door but Lyssa hangs back, pulling me to a large dresser.

"We're going to need cloaks. And something to barter." She pulls a length of dark material from the top drawer of the dresser and a blue velvet bag. From another drawer she grabs a thin journal and slips that into the bag. Lyssa slips on her shoes and turns to me, her expression set. "I'm ready."

We're halfway down the hallway, when I spin back to Lyssa's room. The sound of many footsteps is echoing up the main staircase, between us and the back stairs. We aren't going to make it out that way. Lyssa and Shadow follow me back into the room without question, and we push the dresser in front of the door in silence.

Crossing the room, I throw open both windows. The first reveals a daunting drop onto an iron-tipped fence. The second overlooks a vine-covered arbor. Shadow appears at my side. He puts his paws up on the window sill and looks over the edge then back at me.

"Go," I say firmly.

His mouth falling open in a goofy grin, long pink tongue dangling, Shadow launches himself out the window and onto the lattice of the arbor. Another leap and he is on the ground.

I turn to Lyssa, extending my hand. "You next." Lyssa passes me her bundle of fabric and places her hand in mine, maneuvering her body through the window as the door begins rattling behind us. Lyssa scoots along the ledge under the window as I follow her out. There are shouts and banging coming from outside the bedroom door now, but we stand side by side, for a moment, and contemplate the drop down to the top of the arbor.

"Trust me?" I ask her, holding out my hand.

"With my life," she replies. Lyssa slaps her palm against mine and we step off the ledge, both grinning like madwomen, as the bedroom door crashes open behind us.

Chapter Twenty-Seven

Sitting in her bed and eating sweets, Lyssa and I had talked about escaping on a ship to the colonies. It was the kind of dream you talk about but never actually do. Until it becomes the only option left.

Luckily for me, Lyssa takes these things much more seriously than I do. She also has access to a library full of information about the colonies and the manifests from her father's shipping company. Lyssa has an actual plan.

"There are two ships scheduled to leave port in the morning, one is going north but the other is going to New Hope," she explains as we run through the dark city.

"Is it your father's ship?" I ask.

"He doesn't own it, just the cargo."

Shadow veers down an alley and we both follow him without question. The streets here are narrow and paved with rough stones. I stay close to Lyssa and have to grab her a few times when she trips over the uneven surface. We turn again and again, working our way through the labyrinth of streets and getting closer and closer to the docks. On my way into the city I'd run a straight line and it had seemed so close. But no one was chasing me then.

The moon is high in the night sky by the time we make it to the actual harbor. There is a large metal fence around the docks with a guard stationed at the gate. Warehouses sit on both sides of the fence and we tuck ourselves into the recessed door of a dark loading dock to come up with a plan.

Lyssa is panting slightly from the run through the city and I look at her closely. Her face is pale and her hands are shaking.

"You're hungry."

She nods, wrapping her arms around her middle to ward off the chill. I move closer and Shadow sits on her other side, blocking the cool breeze from the sea.

"I haven't had anything since they tied me up," Lyssa says, huddled between us.

Before she can stop me, I draw a short line across the skin at the base of my thumb. Blood wells up immediately and begins to run down my hand as Lyssa gasps.

"Take it," I tell her.

"Why would you do that?" she hisses at me, covering the wound with her hand and gripping it firmly.

"Don't let it go to waste," I tell her calmly.

Lyssa stares at me in frustration, still clutching my hand around the base of my thumb. Huffing an exasperated breath, she runs the fingers of her other hand along my arm where a line of blood is heading toward the ground. Scooping the drop onto her finger, she places it in her mouth. Again she runs the finger up my arm and wrist, leaving the skin clean and slightly damp.

Carefully, she peels her hand from mine, grimacing at the blood now coating both of our palms. Raising her own hand to her face she makes quick work of cleaning her skin, removing the stain with long strokes of her broad tongue.

When her hand is clean I hold mine out to her. Her color has returned and she is no longer shivering. I won't force her to take this last bit of spilled blood, but it seems silly to waste it.

Without looking at me, Lyssa carefully grasps my hand in both of hers and brings it to her face. She gazes down at it consideringly, then quickly darts her tongue out to lap at the blood pooled in the crease at the base of my thumb. Each pass of her tongue is like a lightning strike and it takes all of my strength not to jump away from the invisible arc of electricity.

Keeping my breathing normal, I tell her, "You look better."

"I feel better," she says. "You're the best medicine."

We huddle together in our little bubble of warm darkness, while the sound of the wind and the faint calls of the guards and the stevedores at the dock echo through the night. I let myself bask in this moment for a little while longer.

Focus, I tell myself. "What is the name of the ship?"

Lyssa frowns. "Moon or midnight something...the *Midnight Runner*!"

"How do we know they will even help us?" I ask, realizing we have more concerns. "We have no money."

"Well," Lyssa begins, "we have two options. There is a chance I can convince them to grant us passage based on my father's lease of their cargo space."

"And the second option?"

"Violence," Lyssa announces succinctly. I like this option but I'm not quite sold on the plan in general.

"What is in the blue bag?" I ask.

"Some of my mother's jewels. Bribery is our backup plan."

I nod. That seems more reasonable than trying to fight our way aboard a ship neither of us knows how to sail. Either way, we need to get out of this city. There is nothing for us here. No one to help, nowhere to hide.

"I've met this captain more than once," Lyssa is saying. "He came to the house to sign the contract with father," she continues. "He came back a couple of days ago and told my father he wouldn't be renewing the contract if he partners with Mannix."

"Did he say why?"

"I couldn't hear the whole conversation, but it sounded like he had some history with Mannix. He was trying to warn my father." Lyssa hesitates, her eyes unfocused. "He was odd, but not in a bad way. I asked my father about him afterward."

"Odd?" Now I am even more concerned. "Like me?"

Lyssa barks out a short laugh and focuses her eyes on me again. "You're not odd!"

I stare at her until she rolls her eyes. "Fine," she huffs. "You're a little odd." Lyssa reaches out and squeezes my hand. "But you're mine and I'm keeping you."

My throat closes and I couldn't say anything even if I knew what to say. So I turn my hand in her grasp and hold on tight. Finally I croak out, "Same," and turn back to the dock.

"How do we find the ship?" I ask, changing the subject.

Lyssa keeps a firm hold of my hand, but follows my lead and turns to contemplate the large fence between us and the dock.

"I think I can climb that," Lyssa says slowly. "Right now I feel like I could fly over it. But what about Shadow?" She turns to look at the wolf crowding us against the doorframe.

I follow her gaze and nearly laugh out loud at the affronted look on my friend's face.

"Shadow won't slow us down," I assure her. "Don't worry about him."

Lyssa shrugs her acceptance. "Then we go over the fence and check each ship. The boat is called *Midnight Runner*. I don't know what it looks like but I don't think it's very big. The captain is a tall man with red hair."

I must have looked at her dubiously, because she squeezes my hand.

"We can do this. There can't be that many ships and we have hours until dawn."

Chapter Twenty-Eight

It turns out that there are a lot of ships. The dock has dozens of long piers reaching out into the bay and each one has perhaps a dozen or more ships attached to it of various sizes. Then we realize there are even more ships anchored in the bay itself.

The hours that we have until dawn race past as we work carefully down each pier, dodging the guards and the few seamen still milling about. My mind is racing, trying to come up with a backup plan. Soon we'll have to either leave the harbor to find a place to hide for the night in the city or randomly pick a ship to try to sneak aboard.

I hate both of these options.

"We're not going to find it," I finally tell Lyssa. The three of us are crouched behind a stack of large crates piled at the entrance of yet another long wooden pier. I gaze down the row of tethered ships, all of them blending together at this point.

"We will," she insists. "We have to."

"I know you don't want to give up, but it's almost dawn." I search her face, committing it to memory.

"This is our only chance. Come on," Lyssa's voice is firm. She grabs my hand to tug me down the pier but I resist, keeping her in our hiding spot.

"This is *your* only chance. Shadow can go with you, but I can't stay," I tell her softly. Lyssa whips her head around to look at me.

"Stop," she says, her eyes blazing as she leans in close to my face. "Don't even say it."

"I have to leave before sunrise, but you can stay and find the ship." I explain to her slowly. Our time has run out.

"We are not separating," Lyssa counters. She enunciates each word clearly as her face moves closer and closer to mine. "Tomorrow we'll come back and find another one."

I sigh. We don't have any more time.

"But this is the ship that you planned on. The one that goes where you want to go," I remind her. "And it will be easier to find in the daylight."

A group of sailors passes our hiding spot and we tuck ourselves further back into the shadows, turning our pale faces into Shadow's fur. As the voices continue down the next pier, I glance after the group.

"If you think—" Lyssa begins.

"You said the captain has red hair?" I interrupt.

Lyssa spins to follow my gaze.

"That's him!" she breathes. "Oh, thank god." Her body sags for a moment and her eyes squeeze shut, tears glinting on her lashes.

Luckily, the docks are busy. There are piles of cargo coming and going, even at this hour of night. Despite the lanterns set at even intervals along each pier, we're able to stay out of sight until we stand before the *Midnight Runner*.

The ship is smaller than most, but built along sleek lines. On the deck the redheaded captain and perhaps a dozen crew members mill about. I glance toward the horizon across the harbor. The sky is already lighter than it had been ten minutes ago. There is no time like the present.

I rise to head toward the ship and Lyssa's hand pulls me back down.

"First, this," she says, handing me the bundle of fabric she brought from the house.

I pull the layers apart to reveal a long midnight blue cloak. I throw the fabric over my shoulders, lifting the hood to cover my face.

"You must keep your head down and your hands hidden in the folds of the cloak," Lyssa instructs.

I nod, understanding.

With Shadow at our side we move out from behind the stack of crates waiting on the pier and approach the ramp leading up to the ship. A young sailor stands guard. His eyes widen at the sight of us, but he calls out in an even voice.

"State your business, Miss."

Lyssa squares her shoulders and continues walking forward. "Please let Captain Felan know that Miss Lyssa Archer requests an audience."

"Please wait on the dock, Miss," the sailor instructs, but Lyssa ignores him and walks up the ramp like a juggernaut, Shadow and I on her heels. The sailor has no choice but to give way as we step onto the deck, which is well-lit with lanterns spaced along the railing. Wooden structures rise from the deck at either end.

Flustered, the sailor hesitates. "Archer?"

"Yes, Archer, as in Archer Shipping. Now run along, my good man, and find me the captain."

He waffles for a minute more before lurching off along the railing, calling for the captain. It isn't a large ship and within seconds an answering shout sounds from the other end of the deck. The same tall, redheaded man we glimpsed earlier comes striding over to confer quietly with his man before joining us where we stand against the railing. He is older than I thought, with a bearded face and surprisingly light eyes that look golden in the light from the lanterns.

Captain Felan moves to stand before Lyssa, looking her up and down. He glances at Shadow, frowning, then over at me, pausing to take a longer look. I refrain from hissing at him and step up closer behind Lyssa, looking down at her shoulder and clutching at the hand she reaches back to me.

"Good morning, Miss Lyssa," the captain says finally. "To what do we owe the honor of this visit?" He arches a hairy eyebrow. "I can't imagine your father sent you here on business."

"No," Lyssa confirms. "I am not here on my father's behalf. I believe you are aware that my father has a new business partner?"

"I am," the captain responds, a wealth of disapproval in the two small words. I have no idea where Lyssa is going with this. I really should have asked more questions before we boarded the ship. I'm still fairly sure she wasn't serious about using violence.

"I had the impression from your last meeting with my father that you were not a fan of Lord Mannix."

The captain's brows lower over those odd golden eyes as he stares down at Lyssa.

"I am not," he says finally.

"Then we have that in common, Captain." Lyssa lifts one hand in a broad gesture to encompass the ship. "I also believe you are departing for the colony of New Hope this morning. Is that correct?"

"What is it that you are doing here, Miss Archer?" the captain cuts in impatiently. "I cannot believe that your father would allow you to be out at this hour without a proper escort."

Lyssa continues as if he hasn't spoken. "I am also bound for New Hope, Captain. Archer Shipping has contracted the entirety of your capacity for this voyage, is that not correct?"

The captain stares at Lyssa, his eyes again moving over me and finally resting on Shadow. He glares at the wolf as if looking for some kind of sign.

Finally the captain sighs. "What is going on here, Miss Archer?"

"You may not be aware, Captain," Lyssa begins, "but my father has promised Lord Mannix my hand in marriage."

Felan rears back, his head moving back on his neck in shock at Lyssa's statement. "He didn't."

"He did." Lyssa counters. "And the ceremony is to take place this very morning. Perhaps you can see why I am currently in need of passage to the colonies?"

The captain doesn't answer for the longest time and my tension builds. He looks again at each of us, his gaze coming back to rest on Lyssa's face. I pull air in and hold it, then let it out, as slowly as I can. All the while, the sailors move around us, readying the ship for its imminent departure.

"Welcome aboard the *Midnight Runner*, Miss Archer."

Chapter Twenty-Nine

Captain Felan shows us to his first officer's cabin. The owner of the room, a short man with a round face, slips past us to gather a few belongings and leaves again without a word of complaint.

"Thank you again, Mr. Yong," Lyssa calls after him.

"Stay in this room until I come to get you," Felan orders, then he too is gone and the three of us are alone in the small room.

I look at Lyssa. "Are we safe?"

"I don't know," she answers, walking to the small round window set in the wooden wall of the room and latching the cover shut tightly. "Probably not," she shrugs. "Mannix or my parents could still find us before the ship sets sail. And even if we make it out of port, we'll be stuck on this ship full of strange men for the better part of a month." Lyssa flops down beside me on the small bed.

She jolts back up as if the bed is on fire. "What will you both eat?" she cries, turning to face us. "I didn't consider your dietary requirements. You can't go three weeks without meat or blood! We must get off the ship before it leaves the dock!"

"We'll be fine! There's plenty of meat on this ship," I assure her.

Lyssa presses her hand over her racing heart. "Are you sure? How can you tell?"

"I can smell it," I tell her. "There must be a ton of cured meat in the hold." I smirk. "I can hear a colony of rats, as well."

"Ew," she responds as expected. "Although I'm sure the captain won't mind you taking care of that problem."

Lyssa settles back onto the bed, leaning against the pillows, lost in thought.

"Once we get to New Hope we'll have to find a place to live, a way to survive."

"What's your plan?" Lyssa always has a plan.

"Well," she starts, "I've reviewed the cargo manifests and growing schedules for the different crops coming from the colonies and we have three good options. We'll put in a homestead claim on a little piece of land and hire at least one hand. If my calculations pan out, then we should be able to double our income within the first two years and buy more land...."

I let her voice drift over me as the rising sun lulls me to sleep.

I wake to the dim light of a single lantern hanging from a bracket by the wall. I'm alone. Wherever Lyssa and Shadow are at the moment, I'm certain that they're together. I'm not panicked, but I want to find them.

I'm also hungry.

Stepping from the room, I follow the narrow passageway to the deck—and stop. It's...bright. I've never seen the world so sharp and light. The sea is reflecting the light of the full moon and the ship is awash in its silver light. Lanterns hang at intervals along the railing as well, but the moonlight is so bright they barely make a difference.

I spin to take in the illuminated world around me and my eyes catch on Lyssa, her back to me as she stands at the railing. Her hair is half up with ringlets falling down her back and it looks like ivory in this light. Shadow is next to her, his paws up on the railing and his head towering over hers.

I've never seen Shadow in such bright light and I take a moment to admire his thick coat and massive paws. His back is a long line, culminating in a tail that sweeps up and curls, lush with glossy black fur.

"They're yours?" asks a voice from beside me and I jump. Captain Felan has come shockingly close.

"Yes," I answer—then remember I'm not supposed to let him see my teeth. I press my lips together, but of course it's too late. I wait for the captain to gasp or scream, but he does neither.

"The girl told me that Mannix is your father," he says instead.

"Yes." I could lie, but what's the point? If we're going to be stuck on this ship for weeks, then he'll know what I am, if he doesn't already.

"She said you offered to take care of our rodent problem." Felan lifts an eyebrow and I shrug one shoulder at him. "Appreciate it," he says and walks away.

I'm left staring after him.

Shaking off my confusion, I start toward Lyssa and Shadow as a cry comes from above. A man in the crow's nest is pointing behind us. I can't make out what he's saying but there's a flurry of activity on the deck. Lyssa is looking around in concern when she spots me and runs over to sweep me into a hug that nearly knocks me off my feet. A strategically placed wolf at my back keeps me upright and I wrap my arms around her shoulders, squeezing her back.

"What's going on?" I pull back enough to ask, dropping a hand to run over Shadow's head.

"They've spotted another ship," Lyssa explains. We share a concerned glance.

"That's not usual, I take it?" Sailors are running across the deck, making adjustments in the sail and calling out commands. Felan is heading our way.

"Get off the deck," he commands abruptly. "We have trouble." The three of us are shepherded back to the cabin I woke up in, Felan on our heels.

"What is going on, Captain?" Lyssa demands. "Is the other ship a hostile?"

"The other ship, Miss Archer, belongs to your father," he announces. "And I think we can both make a very good guess of who might be on board."

"Mannix," Lyssa and I say together, sharing a glance.

The captain nods.

"They have 20 tons on this ship and there's no way we can outrun them. We're going to have a fight on our hands."

"A fight?" Lyssa gasps. "You think they might try to board us?"

"I do, Miss Archer. So please stay in this room and off of the deck. I'll be back for you soon."

Felan turns to leave and I grab his arm.

"I can fight," I tell him, not bothering to hide my teeth or the claws laid across his sleeve.

"I bet you can," he agrees. "But we can handle this one. Stay here and protect Miss Archer. It will be over soon."

He turns again toward the door and Shadow whines, taking a step after him. "Nope," the captain cuts him off. "You stay with the girls, too. If the demon gets past us, you're their last defense."

With that, the captain slams out of the room, leaving all three of us staring at the door. Finally, I turn to Lyssa. "Demon?" I echo.

"He knows," Lyssa confirms. "I suspected as much when I heard him arguing with my father."

"You told him that Mannix is my father," I say. A statement, not a question. "He knows what I am, too."

Lyssa grips my hand, her face tight. "I had to be honest with him, Sharptooth. There's no way we could have kept the secret on this ship."

"I understand. I'm not mad." I squeeze her hand and shrug. "I'm confused, though. He isn't shocked or afraid or anything. I expected more of a reaction."

Lyssa cocks her head. "I noticed too. I suspect Captain Felan—and perhaps his entire crew—are not what they seem." She turns an accusing stare to Shadow, who is lying across the doorway. "And you, sir! Anything you'd like to confess while we're at it?"

Shadow gives a jaw cracking yawn and lowers his head onto his paws, ignoring her completely. Lyssa continues to taunt the beast while I move to open the window.

Peering out the small round hole, I gasp. The other ship is shockingly close. Lyssa hurries to my side and we both stare at the hull that is only a stone's throw away. Shouts fill the air and ropes fly from the attacker and land somewhere above us on the deck. The lines pull taut and we reach for each other as our ship lurches in response.

"They're boarding us!" Lyssa cries, turning toward the door. I follow her as Shadow rises to his feet, still blocking the doorway.

"Felan said to stay here. The crew will handle this." If Mannix is on that ship, I have no desire to see him again.

As Lyssa opens her mouth to respond, the wall behind us splinters apart.

Chapter Thirty

It's dark and everything around me is warm and soft. Below me are strands of smooth, silver hair visible in the moonlight. At my back I recognize the heat radiating from Shadow's big, furry body. Moving carefully away, I realize I'm sandwiched between them. I work a hand up to brush the hair from Lyssa's face to find it slack, her eyes closed.

"Lyssa," I shake her gently. The sound of my own voice brings the other noises around me rushing back. Water is slapping the side of the ship, wind rushing around us, and further away the sound of footsteps and men's shouts echo against the wood deck.

Shadow whines quietly against my back and I run my hands over the back of Lyssa's head, checking for injuries.

"Lyssa, wake up," I say more firmly. Shadow whines again and I shake my shoulders, trying to dislodge him. "Shadow, get off."

Wiggling to get myself out from between them, I look over my shoulder to spur him to action and freeze at the sight of a large wooden splinter protruding from the ball of his shoulder.

Shadow whimpers again and slides off of me onto the wooden deck. I reach out a hand onto his foreleg, moving over him to examine the wound. The splinter is more of a spear. The part sticking out of his fur is as long as my hand and wider than a finger.

"I'm going to pull it out," I tell him. There's the possibility he'll bite me, as a reaction to the pain, but we have no choice. I have no idea what's going on out on the main deck and I'm trying hard not to look at the open side of the room where the outer wall used to be. The attacker's ship is pulled up alongside us, blocking the night sky.

Moving my eyes resolutely to the long wood splinter embedded in Shadow's shoulder, I ignore everything else for the moment. Placing one hand against his fur, I grasp the splinter and pull. It is not easy and the wood eats into my skin, but finally it breaks free and I throw it at the hole in the wall.

I slap my hand down over the wound. We've lost the lantern at some point and the room is dark, but Shadow's black fur is wet with blood. Despite the sting of the cuts on my hand, I find myself once again gazing at the hole in the side of the ship. Besides the splintered edges, the entire wall of the room is gone. Nearly close enough to touch, the hull of the other ship fills the gap, undulating sickeningly.

Forcing my gaze away, I twist around to find Lyssa beginning to stir behind me and I sag a little with relief. Shadow struggles to his feet under my hand and I fight to maintain pressure on his wound. The big wolf shakes me off and moves toward the door, looking back at me expectantly.

I ignore him and kneel beside Lyssa, who is pushing herself off the floor, a hand to her head. I run my hands over her scalp again, searching for any injury or sign of a wound. She catches my hand in her own.

"I'm not hurt," she insists, pushing to her feet.

Shadow is pawing at the door and Lyssa opens it, releasing the big wolf. I want to object. We were supposed to stay in this room. But, of course, this room is literally falling apart around us.

I'm turning to follow Lyssa and Shadow from the room when I catch movement from the corner of my eye. A man swings into the room through the hole where the wall once was. I stare in amazement as he lands before me, a pistol rising in his hand.

Without a thought in my head, I strike out with one clawed hand and the man thuds to the wood floor, unmoving.

The exchange has only taken a matter of seconds but Lyssa is gone when I turn back and I careen out the door after her.

The deck is in chaos. Swords and bodies fly through gunsmoke that drifts in dreamy clouds of moonlight. The *Midnight Runner* is in darkness but the attacker's vessel sports glowing lanterns along the rail that cast a golden glow over both ships.

A sailor runs toward me, the lantern light making his eyes flash yellow-gold and I raise my claws.

He yells, "Down, Miss!" and I duck as a sword sweeps through the space my neck was a moment ago. The sailor before me grabs the arm holding the sword with claws of his own. They sink deep into the flesh and the sword falls to the deck as the man cries out. The sailor flings the invader toward the railing of the ship and he disappears from sight.

"There's a hole in the ship," I tell him for no reason and he stares at me blankly until another attacker comes at him from the side. They roll away from me and a flash of silver hair catches my attention.

Lyssa is braced against the far railing, a pistol in her hands. Shadow is at her feet, tearing the throat from a man dressed in black and red livery.

"What are you shooting at?" I ask when I make it to her side, dodging combatants. Lyssa is aiming at the space between the two ships.

"The ropes," she mumbles, focused on her shot. The blast knocks her back but the rope she aimed at snaps, both ends flying. The ship sways in response, but there are still other tethers and I slash at them with my claws. With each snap both ships shudder and the remaining tethers pull more taut.

Lyssa cries out and I fly to her side, but Shadow has already pinned her attacker to the deck and is gnawing on his head. Without pausing, Lyssa turns back to her task, taking out another rope. With this shot, the entire ship shudders and strains. The remaining tethers snap and the *Runner* lurches away from her attacker, tilting precariously as the sea rushes in between the ships again.

Lyssa's pistol goes flying and she wraps her arms around the railing, her legs dangling over the churning sea. I'm working my way toward her, moving down the railing hand over hand, when Shadow comes sliding past me. I reach out and anchor one hand into the thick fur at the nape of his neck.

Finally the ship rights itself and Lyssa is back over the deck, scrambling to get her feet under her. Shadow digs his long claws into the wood and we both rush to her side.

"He's here," she gasps, reaching for my hand.

"Where?" I don't need to ask who.

"I saw him fighting Felan at the bow." Lyssa is on her feet again, but I still hold onto her.

"The what?"

"The front of the ship!" She points. "That way!" There's a cloud of gunpowder and mist cutting us off from that end of the ship. The flash of pistols firing cuts through the dust along with the odd glimpse of a flying fist or a furry leg. A tail appears for a moment and I glance to make sure Shadow is still by our side. He is.

I don't want to leave Lyssa, but I can't stay here. As I'm waffling, Lyssa takes the decision out of my hands and lurches across the deck. She scoops up a fallen saber and starts into the fog, blade held before her.

A man dressed in Mannix's livery lunges from the mist, pistol raised, and Lyssa brings the saber down across his wrist. The pistol falls to the deck along with his hand as I grab the front of his shirt. He's screaming and his body is sagging so I let him drop to the deck, a bit put out to find myself superfluous.

Shadow pounces on the hand. A moment later he drops the pistol at Lyssa's feet, the hand having disappeared.

"Thank you!" Lyssa gasps as she picks up the firearm. Hefting a weapon in each hand, she sets out across the deck again, the two of us in her wake.

Chapter Thirty-One

It's hard to tell between the billowing clouds of gunpowder and the sea mist that gives everything a fuzzy glow, but it seems like the fight is winding down. The two ships have drifted apart and Mannix's men are splashing into the space between them, desperately swimming for their ride home.

We pick our way over bodies and around combatants still locked in battle as the mist begins to dissipate. The figure that appears before us is a man-wolf. It's tall and broad with the head of a wolf on the frame of a man. Its fingers end in claws not unlike my own and its feet are long like a hare's. Lyssa raises the pistol and the man-wolf holds up a flat hand, palm out, and takes a step back.

Lyssa lowers the pistol and nods as I pull her past him and back toward the front of the ship. We take a moment to exchange a look, but now is not the time. I spare one glance over my shoulder at the beast as he disappears the way we've come and find Shadow doing the same.

From both sides, shapes burst from the mist. Shadow rises up to meet his attacker and I focus on my own. Raking my claws across the man's neck, I'm relieved to note it's another of Mannix's henchmen, as he falls dead to my feet. Shadow stumbles back into view, no one behind him, so his attacker must be vanquished as well. Lyssa stands watching us and we both lunge forward as a figure appears from the mist to wrap his arms around her neck and waist.

"Drop your weapons or I'll break your neck," growls the man. Lyssa struggles to raise the pistol over her shoulder but he has her pinned. I run forward and he wraps one hand around her chin, pulling her neck impossibly tight. "I'll end her," he threatens.

"Then I'll end you," I respond. "What's the point?"

"The point, dear child," a voice cuts through the night like a knife, "is that you can't take things that don't belong to you." Mannix solidifies from the fog, tall and unruffled in his long black cloak.

"Things?" I ask. "Like your arm?" I can't tell what's under the cloak, but I don't believe he could heal an injury like that.

Mannix releases a bitter laugh and shrugs the cloak over his shoulder, revealing an empty sleeve. "I was referring to Miss Archer here, but yes, that too." He steps closer and I tense, ready to spring. "I blame myself, of course. I knew the minute I saw you that you were an abomination that needed to be exterminated. I hesitated and I paid the price."

"I'm not an abomination and Lyssa is not a thing!" I scream at him. "You are a murderer and a demon and I'm not going to let you hurt anyone else."

I prepare to fly at the demon and he sweeps a hand toward his man holding Lyssa.

"Don't forget your little friend. One step toward me and my man will snap her neck." I glance over and Lyssa's neck is still stretched tight, her head held at a high angle by the man behind her. She meets my gaze calmly, lips pressed firmly together.

A growl reverberates through my chest, my mind racing in circles as I try to come up with a plan or strategy.

Lyssa jerks and my heart stops in my chest. The beat resumes as the arms around her fall away and she steps forward as her attacker hits the deck. Behind her, Captain Felan reaches down to retrieve his dagger from the man's back.

I fly at Mannix, claws aimed for his throat.

His arms are longer than mine, though, and I come up short with his hand wrapped around my neck. Swinging my legs forward, I push him away, vaguely aware of the pain as his hand is torn away from my throat. We clash together again and this time I come in under his reach and my own claws slash at his face, opening a line from temple to chin.

Mannix bares his teeth at me and the facade of the gentleman falls away, finally. His eyes are red and his teeth are sharp like mine. Yes, we are the same kind of monster.

"You can't have her," I snarl into his face. I've found the big vein on the side of his neck and I dig in, but my claws are weak. They aren't responding and my vision is growing black around the edges. Mannix chuckles and my blood grows cold.

My face hits the deck and I stare at the wood. There are things happening above me but I'm so cold. Dark droplets appear on the wood, like they did when I woke up in my room after the fire. The fire that Mannix set to kill my mother.

Something soft and warm presses against my cold lips. When I can finally focus, there is a white wrist before my eyes and I breathe in the scent of flowers and cool waters and moonlight. *Lyssa.* I blink and her face is near mine.

"Bite," she's screaming, from far away.

No, not Lyssa.

I close my eyes tight but my teeth get longer and sharper in my mouth. Pain is radiating from my center and the skin of my neck itches as it tries to knit itself back together again.

"Bite," Lyssa whispers, right next to my ear, her voice clear as a bell through my head. "Bite, my darling girl."

Warm, rich blood flavored like sunshine and summer grasses and soft kisses floods my mouth. My eyes are open but the world is a blur of light and sound as every nerve in my body explodes with the power of Lyssa's blood. My skin itches as the wounds on my neck heal, then the wounds on my back and hip I hadn't even been aware of. They all seal close, the skin tight and smooth.

This time when I open my eyes, the world is sharp and crisp. The smoke and gunpowder and mist still hangs in the air but every figure on the ship is visible to me.

I lay Lyssa carefully onto the deck, her face white and still, and turn to where Felan and Mannix are squaring off against each other. Shadow lies on his side at their feet, his chest shuddering and blood covering his muzzle. Felan swings at Mannix with a clawed hand and Mannix kicks him square in the chest, causing the captain to fly backward across the deck.

My eyes flick back to Mannix and he's suddenly within arm's reach.

"Still here, child?" he asks. The veneer of civilization is completely gone now. His eyes are red and his teeth are long and jagged, like knives sticking out of his mouth. This is the monster. But I've hurt him too. Blood coats his neck and chest. I need to finish the job.

This time I don't claw at Mannix's neck—I stab. My fingers dig through skin and sinew and blood spurts in dark waves, newly healed scars tearing open again.

"Die," I growl, sinking my other hand into his chest, digging through fabric and flesh in search of his heart. I'll rip it out and then I'll know he's finally dead. For my mother. For Lyssa. For the woman hanging from the ceiling and everyone else this monster has hurt.

I run through the night in the forest. I am a predator. I am not a monster and I understand the difference now.

The skin around my fingers is getting tight as Mannix struggles to heal the wounds and the blood flow slows. He chuckles, wetly.

"You can't kill me, child," he says and a white form appears behind him.

"Yes, we can," Lyssa corrects Mannix as she wraps her thin white arms around his head and sinks her teeth into the other side of his neck from where my fingers are digging to find his jugular. Her throat works and Mannix's mouth falls open, his eyes wide.

I rip my hand from his throat and bring it down to join my other, digging through his chest. I rip aside yards of black fabric to reveal blood-stained skin, a gaping hole glittering wetly with moving parts. Sinking in both hands to the wrist, I begin pulling out whatever I can grasp.

There it is! The smooth, pulsing muscle of Mannix's heart is laid bare. I grab it with both hands and pull with all of my might. With a squelch it releases and I fly back onto the deck, hands tight around my trophy.

Mannix drops like a stone to the deck, Lyssa riding his body down. She disengages from his neck, releasing his head so that too can flop onto the wood. Lyssa and I are left staring at each other, covered in blood and grime.

"He's gone," she says, crawling toward me.

She grabs at my hands and then we are in each other's arms. She's the only thing holding me together as sobs begin to wrack my body. Mannix is dead. He was my father and he is dead. My mother is dead. She didn't leave me. He killed her. He's dead. I've been alone for so long. Now I'm really an orphan, but I'm not alone.

I rear back. "Your teeth!"

Lyssa laughs, and I stare in wonder. They're small, but they're sharp, like mine. I can also see the tears on her face, which are red.

"I don't understand," I tell her, but I can feel the smile on my face.

Chapter Thirty-Two

Untethered from Mannix's ship, the *Midnight Runner* is moving quickly through the water again and leaving the gunsmoke and fog behind. Through the clearing air Lyssa and I spot Felan and Shadow struggling to their feet and scramble to help. The captain has blood running down the side of his head and an arm facing the wrong way. Shadow has multiple gashes across his body, but he's breathing easily and is able to stand.

As Lyssa is fussing over the big wolf, a sailor and I help the captain force his arm back into the socket with a wet pop.

"I told you three not to leave the cabin," he says blandly. Eying the blood covering each of us.

"It exploded," I inform him, lifting my eyebrows. "There's a big hole in the side of your boat." The captain flinches and strides off without another word.

At the far side of the deck, one of Mannix's men is being forcefully helped over the railing, landing with a scream and a splash. On both sides of the ship sailors are dumping red and black-uniformed bodies over the side and helping their injured shipmates to their feet. Mannix's body is pushed into the sea. His ship is nowhere in sight.

"They're werewolves," Lyssa says, nodding toward a pair of crew members limping toward the other end of the ship. One is the man-wolf I'd seen during the fight. As we watch, his fur recedes into his skin to reveal the young sailor who had met us when we approached the *Runner*.

I glance down at Shadow, who is also staring intently after the man.

"You knew?" I ask him.

He flicks his eyes up at me and settles back down at my side.

At that moment Felan strides back on deck, throwing orders to the men around him. In short order the deck is cleared, the wounded are tended to, and a team is hanging over the side, repairing the gaping hole where our room used to be. Finally, the captain is free to turn his attention back to us.

Striding to where Lyssa, Shadow, and I are huddled against the base of the main mast, Felan stands over us, arms crossed. We are quite a mess. Shadow looks the best, his black coat hiding wounds and bloodstains. Lyssa and I have made a feeble effort to clean up our faces, but we're both filthy and once again my dress is in tatters.

"How are you, Captain?" Lyssa asks politely.

"Fine, thank you, Miss Archer. And you?" the captain responds, arms still crossed over his chest.

"Well, I appear to be quite dead, but otherwise fine," Lyssa responds archly.

The captain scoffs at her. "Now, now, Miss Archer. I know you are a well read young lady. I'm sure you don't put stock in such myths and misconceptions. You are no more dead than I am."

"And no more human than you are?" Lyssa probes.

"Indeed," the captain nods. "If you three would accompany me to my cabin, I think it's time to clear the air."

It takes rather more effort than it should for Lyssa and me to drag ourselves to our feet. We're both shaking by the time we settle into chairs around the captain's table. Shadow flops down under our feet and is asleep almost immediately.

"You've been giving Lyssa your blood?"

I whip my head up and Felan is examining me from his seat across the table. I nod, not knowing where he's going with this line of questioning.

"That explains her miraculous recovery—and subsequent resurrection."

"Resurrection?" Lyssa interrupts. "Then I was dead."

"Near death," the captain corrects. "The two of you have pulled off a very difficult, very rare feat."

"Lyssa is like me now?"

To my dismay, the captain shakes his head. "Not quite." He gazes at me consideringly. "Your mother was Amelia?"

"Yes," I gasp. "You knew her?"

"You look like her." The captain pushes his chair back and begins to pace the room. "I only met your mother once. She was from the city." The captain pauses to look at me. "You're a dhampir. A half-breed."

"Mannix was a vampire." Lyssa doesn't phrase it as a question but the captain nods anyway.

"Yes, most likely the last of his kind...until you." I hate the way the captain frowns at Lyssa, as if she's a problem dropped into his lap.

"How can a dhampir turn someone into a vampire?" Lyssa asks. "That should be impossible."

"Yes," the captain agrees, frowning down at us and crossing his arms over his chest. Finally, the man sighs and resumes his pacing. "Regardless, it has happened. Maybe someone in New Hope will be able to give you more answers."

"So there are more people like us in the colonies?" Lyssa confirms. "I was quite sure that was the case, from reading between the lines in the journals I've accessed." Her eyes light up with research-related excitement.

"Yes, that's where most of us have fled. It wasn't safe on the mainland anymore, with Mannix on the rampage." The captain shakes his head. "You don't know how lucky you three were. This was our last voyage. One more day and you would have had a much harder time making it to any of the colonies, much less New Hope."

"Can you tell me more about my mother?" I ask, less interested in what hasn't happened than what has. "You said I look like her?"

The captain sighs and sinks back into his chair across from me. His eyes search my face, my hair, and I need to know if he sees her in me.

"Yes, you look like her," he finally answers, his voice softer. "Her eyes, her hair, the structure of her face. You look like Amelia."

My eyes sting and I reach up to wipe away the tear that runs down my cheek then hold up my red-stained hand to show him. "But not her tears."

"No, not her tears," the captain sighs. "Her tears ran clear like water the one time I met her." Felan clasps his hands before him on the table and stares down at them. "Mannix captured a friend of mine. I went in to rescue him and found your mother had already done the job. I tried to get her to leave with us, but she refused. I think I understand why now."

"Because of me?" I guess, pain spearing through my heart.

The captain nods. "You would have been an infant." Felan's eyes focus back on me. "I'm sorry I didn't do more to help her. We were in the process of moving the last of the wolves from the forest and there were people depending on me."

Suddenly, Felan pushes his chair back from the table to glare at Shadow, curled around my feet. "Which brings us to you, my friend."

Chapter Thirty-Three

Despite Shadow's inability or refusal to shift his form, Felan remains convinced that he is one of them. The rest of the crew seems to concur, and treats him accordingly. Every evening after joining the sailors for their dinner—which consists primarily of meat—Shadow comes to wake me and Lyssa. The three of us climb down to the very bottom of the ship where we decimate the *Midnight Runner*'s rat population.

Despite the damage the ship took during the battle, she makes the crossing to New Hope in record time. Soon I am standing on the deck beside Lyssa, who is bouncing with excitement.

"Can you see it?" her cute little fangs glint in the moonlight as she smiles, hands clasped before her.

"Your eyes are as good as mine," I tell her, shaking my head and hiding my own smile. "Let's move to the front of the ship."

"The bow," Lyssa corrects me for the millionth time, laughing.

We make our way up to the tip of the ship, where the railing forms an arrow, aimed at our new home. There is the faint shadow of land in the distance.

Lyssa pushes herself into the vee of the railing, leaning forward into the wind.

"Be careful," I tell her, grabbing her waist before she can topple into the sea.

Completely ignoring me, Lyssa steps up onto the bottom edge and braces herself, with her hips against the edge, flinging open her arms as she leans out over the waves. I wrap my arms against her waist, holding myself tight against her back.

Lyssa is laughing into the wind and her heart is beating under my cheek. I'm terrified, and my face hurts from smiling.

"I can see it!" she cries, her voice snatched away by the wind. She pushes back from the railing and steps down. I release my deathgrip on her waist and she turns in my grasp, flinging her arms around me.

"We made it," Lyssa whispers into my neck.

"We made it." I don't know what the future holds, but I know we will face it together and that's enough for me.